THE HUNTER'S FATE

Kade Winter

contents

Chapter 1

You never know when your life is going to change, either for better or for worse. I definitely don't know on Monday the 9th of October, 2073. For all I know I have a boring class with a boring teacher, Mr. Kowis. He's ranting about world explorers, except today he is occasionally glancing back behind him, straight at me. I always shift uncomfortably when he does. My friend, Elsie, notices this and snickers.

"Looks like Mr. Kowis can't look away from you, Stella." She smirks. I snort and nudge her back.

"He might be looking at you," I insist, though I know he's staring at me. If I'm being honest, I'm really uncomfortable. I mask it behind nonchalance.

Mr. Kowis looks back again at me, and looks me up and down once more. Without fail, Elsie giggles. He looks back at the board and starts writing a new sentence. Elsie turns to me and has a smug look on her face.

"So," she whispers, twirling her hair, "you want to hang with me after school? There's this really cute sweater I have that I think would look so cute with those jean-"

"Elsie!" Mr. Kowis shouts. "Would you like to come up here and explain what's so funny?"

"No, Mr. Kowis," Elsie says. She rolls her eyes and looks back to the whiteboard. I do too, but when Mr. Kowis spins toward the board, Elsie looks at me with a raised brow. I raise my eyebrows back.

She sighs and opens her notebook. She hunches over it and writes something out. In small lettering towards the top is "skip?" I nod. She smiles and raises her hand

"Hey, Mr. Kowis?" she asks when he spins around. "Can I go to the bathroom?" When Mr. Kowis nods toward the pass, Elsie stands up and crosses to the front of the classroom, where she grabs one of the rectangle blocks with "Kowis" carved into it. As soon as she's gone, my hand shoots up. He looks at me, and I point to the door.

"Can I go grab my binder from my locker? I need it to take notes." We both know that's a lie, but he sighs dramatically and turns back to the board.

"Quickly, Estelle," he grumbles, using my full first name.

I stand up and go to the remaining block, grab it, and walk out the door.

Elsie's waiting for me in the hall, her blonde hair cascading down her shoulders as she watches me come toward her. We walk to the locker bay to make sure no one's watching.

"Alright, you need to give me the details on your eyeliner. It looks so good today, like literally perfect. Have you been using something different?"

"Actually, yes," I say. "It's this really smooth new stuff I got from-" Footsteps cut me off. I tip-toe-run down the hall, with Elsie on my heels. I go away from the footsteps, and into the bathroom. The steps come closer and closer, until they pass the door, and fade off into the distance.

The bathroom is basic, pretty much every high school bathroom ever. There's obviously some dirty stalls and gross things seen in here that you won't find anywhere else on this green earth.

I go to the mirror to check my reflection. My chocolate brown skin is flawless as always, and my brown eyes are perfectly framed with eyeliner and mascara. My frizzy black curls are in a big ponytail, the front two strands braided, and clips to top it all off. I have a black choker on with a heart dangling off the center. I straighten my black crop top, and stand back to look at how it pairs with my high-rise jeans.

"Okay, real talk now," Elsie says, interrupting my mirror-sesh, "Do you like anyone in this school?"

"No," I answer a bit too quickly. "If there was anybody in this school who was cute to me, I would already have them wrapped around my finger."

The truth is that I think a bunch of people were cute. Like that Leo guy or Jason.

"Uh-huh," Elsie deadpans "Like that one kid in freshman year? He sure liked you."

"That's different," I snap. "I had no experience. I'm a junior! I got this in the bag."

"Alright then," Elsie says. "Pick any one guy in the school, and have him fall for you. Once you do, have him say that he loves you in front of me, so I know for sure. Then, dump him, be a heartbreaker, and I'll believe everything you just said. If not, there is no way to prove anything."

I think for a minute. Would this get me into trouble later? I do really want to prove this to Elsie for some reason. I'm not really the type of girl to hurt somebody, though.

I grumble something unintelligible and glare at her. "Fine. Whatever. Deal." I'm not planning to keep this bet. I hope she'll forget about it in a few days.

Elsie smirks like a cat, which is really not looking good for that whole forgetting thing, and she holds out her hand. Reluctantly, I shake it. Elsie's blue eyes observe me for a second longer, then she drops my hand.

She turns and smacks her bag on the counter by the sink, immediately breaking the tension. She starts digging around inside, then pulls out a vape and turns it on. She takes a hit and offers it to me. I promptly decline.

I've never seen the appeal of vaping, it literally damages your lungs. Plus, it's not the 20s anymore. I don't see why, but people have started to bring vapes back, as disgusting as they are.

She puts it away and digs around in her bag some more, triumphantly pulling out a makeup bag from the bottom. She unzips the makeup bag and gets some mascara. Unscrewing the lid, she leans into the mirror and starts reapplying it. "So, what's the deal with Mr. Kowis? Why did he keep looking at you in class?"

Sighing, I lean against the sink next to Elsie's. "How am I supposed to know? He's creepy, I can tell you that much. And really boring. Almost fell asleep in his class twice today. Honestly, can't he shut up for once?"

Giggling, Elsie screws the lid back on her mascara and puts it back in the bag, pulling out some blush instead. "I don't think that's in his 'vocabulary' or whatever."

I laugh and turn toward the mirror, grabbing some of Elsie's mascara. I start to open the lid but stop, hearing something in the hall. Elsie must have heard it too, because she turns to me and grabs the mascara from my hand. Turning toward the stalls, she bolts inside the one nearest the door and shuts the stall behind her. I take the stall furthest from the door and I lock it behind me. Knowing what to do from skipping so many times, I hop onto the toilet and balance on the seat, trying not to slip. To my horror, the door to the bathroom opens. Heavy footsteps thudded toward my stall. I hope that it's a student.

"I know you're in there, Estelle Booker. Come on out," the intruder says. I inwardly groan. How did they know I was in there? If there were security cameras, they would have picked up Elsie, too. Why were they only going after me?

"If you don't come out, I will resort to force!" The voice yells. I weigh my options. Either go out there and surrender, or stay in here and wait for them to find me. What did force involve, anyway? I probably don't want to find out.

Sighing, I step off the seat and walk to the locked door. Unlocking it, I open the door and glare. It's a security guard. He has gelled hair and a slightly crooked nose with freckles.

"Alright, you got me, sorry, whatever." I hold my hands up in surrender. "What's my punishment?"

Smirking—it's an ugly smirk—the security guard runs a hand through his already smoothed-back hair. "Detention. I'll let Mr. Kowis choose how long to put you in for. Until then, come on. I'll escort you back to your class."

Groaning, I watch as the guard approaches the door. He swings it open and looks back at me, motioning to come along.

"Aren't you forgetting something?" I ask, glancing toward Elsie's stall. The guard doesn't seem to care about my eye movements.

"Nope," he replies. "Now hurry up, you're slowing down my shift."

CHAPTER 2

You never know when your life is going to change, either for better or for worse. I definitely don't know on Monday the 9th of October, 2073. For all I know I'm in gym class, doing push-ups with the other girls. My shoulder-length black hair keeps getting in my face, and I start to wish I had put it in a pony-tail before this. Sighing, I stop, sit up, and tuck my hair behind my ears. Coach Brockney blows her whistle, probably at me. I look up at the coach and roll my eyes at her, then go back to doing push-ups. Finally, after what feels like hours, Coach Brockney claps for everyone's attention. I look up at her, and Coach looks at me for a moment, then writes something down on a piece of paper. Then she looks back up and tells the class in her scratchy voice, "Everyone come report to me how they did. I want nothing but honesty, so you better give it to me."

I mumble something under my breath "Got something to say, Rain?" Coach asks me. "No, Coach," I reply. "Good, now hustle on up here everybody. I don't want any pushing or shoving!" she says with her heavy southern accent. Everyone stands up and lines up in front of her cart with the squeaky wheel she pushes around everywhere. I take my place in the back. The line slowly moves forward until I'm the last on left. I step forward and look at Coach. "How many'd you get?" she asks. "Nineteen," I say. "That's one below the deadline. You're going to get docked points because of that."

I guffaw. I feel my short temper flare. The coach looks at me from the corner of her eye.

My jaw drops. "Wait, you're actually going to dock me points because I didn't do one push up? That's stupid." "Are you back-talking me?" Coach asks with a withering glare. "No, I'm stating my opinion. My opinion is that that's the dumbest thing I've ever heard." Coach turns toward me fully and stares. "If you disrespect me one more time, you're getting detention." I sigh and wander back to my spot on the floor. The last thing I need is to be put in detention tonight, especially since my dad is going to be home for the first time in two weeks from a business trip. I plop back down and look at the Coach. "Next, we're going to be doing some pull-ups. Go to the bars at the back of the room. I'll time you like always with a full minute. The minimum you need is ten."

I go to the makeshift bars in the back, a few girls giggling at me from the small scene I caused. I line up with one of the bars and do a small stretch.

"Starting... now." I hop up and grab the bar with my hands. I pull my body up, touching the bottom of my chin to the top of the pole. I go back down and do one more. Then another. Another. Three down, seven to go. I get up to the bar one more time, but as I'm going down my arms scream at me. Going more slowly this time, I do my fifth one, but time is running out quickly.

My arms hurt really badly, and I'm not sure I can go up one more time. I don't care about points getting taken away that much, so I drop to the ground.

"Ms. Farley!" Coach yells at me. "One more fall and you're getting detention. Stop that attitude and get hustling! Fifteen seconds left!"

Realizing this, I immediately go back to the pole and do one more, then hang there for a second, mentally screaming at my arms and sending all my energy into them. I pull myself up one more time. I'm there for about three seconds, but I can't bring myself to pull up another time. The timer alarm goes off, and I thank God as I get off the pole. Sighing, knowing I am going to be sore tomorrow, I walk away from the pole.

"You know the drill, come on, hurry up," Coach announces. Everybody runs into place in line, me once again in the back, and the line moves. Girls are bragging to each other about their numbers and how they aren't in any pain at all, though I can read facial expressions and can almost always tell if someone is lying. They all are. My dad works as a lawyer, so he teaches me some things. When I finally get to the front of the line, Coach is looking at me funny.   "How many?" she asks, searching my face. I think for a moment. A split second. I decide I am going to lie, say I got ten when I really got seven. I'll have to control my facial expression so Coach won't know I'm lying. Control your heartbeat. Don't break eye contact. I'm an expert at the poker face. "Twenty," I say, not too fast but not too slow. "You're lying," Coach says. "How did you-" I have to physically bite my tongue to stop myself. "I counted," Coach informs. "You're a good liar though, I will give you that. I was considering just docking points and not giving you detention, but since you lied to me..." I stare at her, slack-jawed. "Bu-" "Do I make myself clear?" Coach spits out. I flinch. "Yes, ma'am." "Good. Go back to your seat and don't make another mistake this class period. Don't want to add more days than that one already."

CHAPTER 3

You never know when your life is going to change, either for better or for worse. I definitely don't know on Monday the 9th of October, 2073. For all I know I'm in a chemistry class, doing an experiment with liquids I forgot the names of. I'm wearing goggles and a lab coat, although the experiment isn't that dangerous in the first place. My friend, Xavier, is doing the experiment with me, but he isn't paying attention either. He's swirling the mixture around in the glass when he suddenly stops, looks at me, and smiles. "What?" I ask, half paying attention, half zoning out. "Did you hear Jessie?" he asks. "He's going to pour the mixture out onto the table. You can't let him outdo you, Z!"

It was a ritual at this point, that whenever somebody was in the same class as me, somebody would have to pull a prank on the teachers or another student, resulting in me having to outdo that prank. If I don't, I owe the original pranker two dollars. So far, only two misbehaviors have been so bad, even I couldn't fathom doing worse. One kid actually brought a gun to school for the sake of a prank. I had to mail him two dollars after he got expelled.

All at once, Jessie's concoction falls to the floor, shatters, and he very-fakely gasps. The teacher, Ms. McClair, rushes over and looks at me first, then at Jessie. Looking confused, the teacher walks over to Jessie's mess and starts cleaning it up. Once she gets done, she gets up and glares at Jessie, then tells him to go sit down and be done for the experiment and that he would get a zero. Grinning, Jessie goes back to his seat and plops down.

He turns toward me and raises his eyebrows, as if to say "beat that." I run a hand through my blond hair with a sigh. I was really hoping I wouldn't have to do anything like that today. Guess I'd just have to get detention for the third time this week. But what would I do to outdo him?

"Hey, Xavier," I catch his attention from Jessie, who is now on his phone, very indiscreetly. "What, Z?" Xavier asks. That had been my nickname from day one. Ever since then it stuck with basically everybody. "What's in this stuff?" I look at the concoction in the beaker. It's mostly clear, a little bit bubbly, and really cold. "No clue," Xavier says. "I would ask McClair, but she would just get mad at us for not paying attention." I turn to the front of the classroom, where Ms. McClair is observing the students from her desk.

When her eyes lock on mine they narrow at me. She holds my stare for a second longer before looking at a new kid. I frown and look back at the mixture. Maybe I could spill it too, just this time on Xavier? No, that's too much like Jessie's prank. I at least have to be somewhat original. I could add something else into the mixture that would make it explode? That wouldn't work if I didn't know what was in it already. It was worth a shot though, I would just have to think of something that was fool proof with every substance. Sugar made lots of things bubble up, right? So maybe with this it could work? Without second- guessing myself, I waltz to the middle table, where most of the supplies are kept, and snatch up a sugar packet sneakily. Walking around the table and back toward the lab station, I smirk at Xavier.

"What you got?" Xavier asks, peering at my closed hand. "You'll see," I say, ripping the top off the sugar packet. As fast as I can, I pour the sugar into the beaker and toss the packet onto the floor. I turn my attention back to the mixture, waiting. Waiting. Waiting. "Is something supposed to happen?" Xavier asks after a minute. I groan and glare at the mixture. If only I could think of something, anything, to do before this class period is up. I run through the general idea of getting in trouble, the normal things to get sent to detention for. Class disruption, not completing homework, not participating, being obnoxious, eating in class.... Eating.

That's when it hits me. Eating in class, especially when there are chemicals, is a big no. It was a genius idea, except I don't have any food. "Xavier," I say, trying to be quiet. "Do you have any food?" Xavier looks over at me. "Uhm, no, I don't. You could ask another kid though." I grumble and look around at the other teens. They're all half working, half looking at me, waiting for me to top Jessie. I don't even know if this can top Jessie. I could always go with the natural high-pitched scream. Or the fake fight between him and Xavier.

Except those were just boring and repetitive. Same thing, over and over again. I look over at the mixture one more time, then I stop. The perfect idea. Without time to doubt myself, I pick up the mixture and open my mouth. As quickly as I can, and hoping and praying all the ingredients are edible, I pour the thing in my mouth and swallow it. It was disgusting. So bitter. I gag and the class bursts out laughing.

Ms. McClair runs up to me and grabs the beaker from my hand, placing it on the table. "Go straight to the nurse's office and explain to her what you did!" she says sternly. "Then, once you're done, come back here and stay seated until the end of class! I'm incredibly disappointed in you, Mr. Montes!" With that, she storms off to the front of the classroom and calls up the office on her phone. I grin and head toward the door, laughing at Jessie's shocked and amused face. Jessie whips out his phone and takes a picture of me leaving. A while later in the hall, a ding from my phone confirms that Jessie has posted the picture and tagged me.

CHAPTER 4

Y ou never know when your life is going to change, either for better or for worse. I definitely don't know on Monday the 9th of October, 2073. For all I know I'm in class, next to some very chatty girls.

I try to listen to the teacher, Mrs. Sephin, but the girls' voice grates in, disrupting my attention. I roll my eyes and try to focus, but instead I tune into the girls' gossip.

"So, you know how I wasn't here for, like, all of last week?" she whispers, pausing for dramatic effect as the other girl makes a sound of approval. "It's because my entire house was infested with Hellhounds! Can you believe that? We had to go to a hotel and wait while those little demons tore up our whole house! They even got one of my favorite jackets! I literally cannot believe it still."

The other girl gasps. "Was it that new group? The Red Raiders, or something?"

"No, Red Riders, and yes, it was them! That one guy, the tall one? I don't know what he looks like, but I know for certain he is so hot! Ugh, I can't believe I was gone while he was at my house! Do you think he liked it?"

I zone out and instead think about the poor Hunters that are just trying to do their jobs.

IDHS stood for International Demon Hunting Society, even though they deal with a lot more than demons. Nobody knows much about them, only that they're there in the background, monitoring everything. You call them whenever you have any paranormal or scary activity, sort of like that old movie, Ghostbusters, except they were kind of off.

There are a bunch of these groups, called Hunters, that come into houses and get rid of all the demons and ghosts there. There are some theories that there's a huge place underground that all the Hunters go to train. Also theories that it's in the sky, or in space. The last one was extra ridiculous.

The most reasonable theory was that they used Area 51 for IDHS, but there was no way to tell for sure, even before the Outbreak of the Underworld. The other girl starts talking about skipping class, and I almost sigh in relief. I also somewhat hope that they don't leave the school on their own, because there could be some monsters outside.

A part of the reason it's so bad to skip school and go outside is because of the demons and ghosts out, but they can't get past the Public Barriers anyway, most of the time. The Public Barriers are huge domes that seal everything shut, not letting anything go in or out. But, of course, if the IDHS was there, then the domes aren't absolutely safe. Sometimes they get holes in them from time or from the demons themselves.

The teachers and parents have a basic knowledge of Ghost Hunting because they have to protect the kids, but not any level of training like the Hunters. The two types of Hunter teams are Undercover and Full-Time. From what we do know about IDHS and from speculations, we've figured out that every Hunter group starts off as Undercover, and once they get to a certain age or requirement of some kind, they can either go Full-Time or go Undercover some more.

Sometimes I wonder if I should try out to be a Hunter, then I get my common sense back. There's this whole trial people go through to get in, and from what people say, the trials are so hard that barely any new groups come out of them, ever, so the Red Riders were an interesting bunch. They seemed to appear out of nowhere and they've been deadly and rapid-fire ever since. A voice saying my name pulls me back to the present.

Mrs. Sephin is staring at me. I clear my throat. "Yes, ma'am?" I ask. "Were you paying attention?" she looks at me expectedly. I look to my right and notice that the girls are gone. The board is empty and every head is looking toward me. "Uhm, no, ma'am," I respond. She sighs an exasperated sigh. "What was Charles Dickens' greatest achievement in his life?"

I've never been good at English, just barely keeping an A in this class is hard enough without an insufferable teacher and annoying, snobby kids sitting right smack beside me. I rack my brain but can't come up with anything.

"Uhm, his books?" I venture.

"Which. Ones."

"The...The one that's the most recent?"

"No, Milo, it was not The Mystery of Edwin Drood, although that one is the most notable. To me, atleast."

I just look at her.

"It was arguably Great Expectations. From its intricate characters and in-depth coming-of-age story, it explores class in society and friendships. I'd appreciate it if you would pay attention next time, Mr. Maeda."

"I'm sorry, ma'am, but the girls next to me-"

"Don't put blame on other students, especially when they're not here. You're back talking as well. Do you need to get detention?"

"No, ma'am, it's just also that I don't think you should let the girls that were by me go out-"

"Milo Maeda!" she shouts. "What are you accusing?" "Miss, I just think that you should check-"

"Detention!" she shouts, her cheeks getting red.

Great. She well and truly hates me now.

CHAPTER 5

I arrive in detention first, millions of thoughts running through my head. After what happened in the bathroom that day, the guard seemingly not noticing Elsie, my head jumped to hundreds of conclusions, as it usually tends to do.

I head to the very back and sit in the seat in the middle, a perfect view of the room, and an olive skinned man sitting at the desk in the front. He has glasses, fluffy brown hair, and a friendly face. When his gaze finds mine, he smiles, showing off dimples. He sports a cream sweater with a green jacket. His glasses catch in the light, blinding me. I look away and toward the empty board. The guy looks strangely familiar. Racking my memory, I watch him out of the corner of my eye, and a white girl walks in. I look toward her. She doesn't look familiar, which means I don't have any classes with her. Thick, slightly wavy, cropped black hair with curtain bangs frame a pale face with dark brown eyes.

She has a zip-up black hoodie on and black leggings. She stops, looks over the room once, and her eyes dart back to me. She looks away quickly and takes the seat closest to the door. I watch her back as she puts her bag on the floor and props her left elbow onto the desk, holding her chin in her hand. I look over at the teacher, who is watching the new girl. He looks down and writes something on a sheet of paper. Marking attendance? Then he looks back up and once again meets my gaze. I reach down for my bag and dig through it, embarrassed. Finding what I'm looking for, my phone, I discreetly pull it out and check my notifications. A few new texts from Elsie and notifications from social media. Going with Elsie, I tap her notification and my screen lights up with our messages. Three new ones.

Did u really get detention??Y didnt they come for me??U there????

While thinking of something to say back, a new person walks in. A white boy with blond, messy hair and green eyes struts through the door. I recognize him.

Zain Montes, or Z. The troublemaker of the school. I haven't seen him in person before now, just online. In fact, just today a kid posted him walking out of the classroom. Apparently he drank something from his chemistry class. He's grinning like an idiot, for some reason happy to have detention. He wears a white shirt that parts at the top, turning into a collar. I didn't think out of all the detention classes in the school they would be put together. He looks around the room, just like the girl up front did, but when his gaze meets mine and passes, he does a double take. He goes to the far back corner of the classroom, sitting down in his seat and putting his feet up on the desk. I look back to my phone. I decide to keep my message short.

I have no clue whats going on

Instead of explaining further, I put my phone back in my bag. Hearing footsteps at the front of the classroom, I look up. An asian boy with thick, fluffy black hair and dark eyes walks in. He has a black hoodie with red writing on the sleeve, probably in another language, and black jeans. His eyes rove around the room, and unlike Zain, he doesn't do a double take at me. He just sits down smack in the middle of the classroom.

The teacher, presumably done taking atten- dance, stands up and walks to the front of the room. He looks around at all of us and, deeming what he sees satisfactory, walks to the front of the room. I stare, trying to figure out where I know him from. It seems obvious, like it was on the tip of my tongue. "Alright class," he says. "My name is Mr. Matthews. Today you're in detention because you've gotten into trouble. I'm going to punish you by putting you in here and...hoping you've learned your lesson. We will... uhm... work on any missing work or assign- ments you have to do." He turns back to his desk and sits down.

"That's it?" Zain asks. "Aren't you supposed to, I don't know, punish us?" Seeming to think about this, Mr. Matthews scratches his neck. "I suppose the attic needs some cleaning. Alright then, everyone, follow me. Be silent in the halls." He stands up and walks out the door. We all pick up our bags and follow him. We walk down the hall in silence. I didn't even know the school had an attic, and it seems the kids around me didn't know either. We follow Mr. Matt- hews down the hallway. When we finally get to a dead ended, empty hallway after many twists and turns, Mr. Matthews reaches up toward the ceiling and pulls a cord.

A staircase comes down from the ceiling and Mr. Matthews steps back, letting it smack the floor noisily. He starts to ascend the staircase, taking them two at a time. Zain's next, hands in his jean pockets, striding up the staircase. The girl hesitantly steps forward, almost tripping on the second step as she walks up. I move forward and onto the first step. They're old and rickety and they feel like they could collapse at any second.

I get to the top and step into the dimly lit attic. The room is about the size of any normal classroom, except the ceilings are slanted and there are dusty shelves, a few chairs, and tables scattered around. The attic looks like the place where they shove things that didn't really belong in the storeroom or in the classrooms. It was desperately in need of a clean, which I guess was why we were there.

The dark-haired boy comes up behind me, and I step to the side to give him more room. We are in a circle in the middle of the attic, Mr. Matthews is the farthest away from the exit while I am the closest. He looks around one last time and smiles. "Alright everyone, get cleaning!" He goes to the corner of the room, sits on a chair, and looks at us. I shift my weight awkwardly from foot to foot and look around for cleaning supplies. I don't see any, and the girl seems to notice this at the same time I do. "With what?" she demands. She seems annoyed at his behavior. Mr. Matthews looks around, as if just realizing there's nothing to clean with. "I don't know, figure it out, I guess."

She grumbles something unintelligible and walks over to the shelves, where she swipes at one with her sleeve. She pulls it back with her sleeve covered in dust. She pats it on her pants aggressively, dust raining down onto the floor. She continues this process again, glaring at the shelves. "Well, what are you all waiting for?" Mr. Matthews says. "Make like spring and get cleaning." He laughs as if he had made a hilarious joke. "Get it, because her name is Rain? Rain happens in the spring? No?" Rain. That's the girl's name. Easy enough to remember. Walking toward the shelves, I realize I'll have to use my bare arm to wipe the shelves because I don't have a jacket or sleeves.

Picking a spot at the very back of the room, the farthest away from the door and Mr. Matthews, I half-heartedly start sweeping off the dust with my hand. Zain and the other boy take their places at the shelves toward the front of the room. Realizing hiding back here is the perfect place to observe, I peer over the shelves at Mr. Matthews. There's something about him. Something that just screams familiar. I still have no idea what. His hair is normal-looking, same with his glasses. The more I stare, the more confusing it gets.

I decide to go with a different approach. His name. I abandon my post at the back of the room and make a bee-line toward Mr. Matthews. Mr. Matthews, visibly confused, sits up a little straighter and clears his throat.

"Stella?" he wonders. "What is it?"

"What's your first name?" I ask firmly.

A pause. "Why?" Mr. Matthews shifts uncomfortably in his seat. "Tell me."

"That's not really on a need-to-know basis, is it?"

"No, but I want it to be."

Mr. Matthews looks almost worried. "It's John."

"He's lying," Rain jumps in, stepping around the shelves. "I can tell. Avoiding eye contact."

"Matthews..." I muse aloud. "That name seems... almost familiar." I pinch the bridge of my nose. "Matthews...Ma-" The answer hits me like a brick. "Alexander Matthews."

"What?" Zain asks, leaving the shelf too. "Who's that?"

"He's a famous Hunter," the other boy says, the one with black hair.

I nod. "One who has a full-time job there. Definitely not an Undercover Hunter. So, the question is, what's he doing as a detention teacher at a public high school?"

"I, uhm, well, the thing is," his eyes dart around the room, "I got fired?" His voice is squeaky.

"If he was fired," the boy says, "it would be all over social media. They announce these things, right?"

"Seriously, something is going on. Tell us. Now." I take a step closer, trying to look more intimidating.

Looking around the room one last time, Mr—no—Alexander sighs and hangs his head. "I was really expecting to last longer." He picks his head up and looks at us. "The thing is, the reason why I'm here is really a secret. You have to swear not to tell anyone. If you do, we will find out, and we will erase your minds. That's all I'm telling you, you can ask questions after I'm done explaining."

We look at each other. We obviously weren't expecting this, even though it was probably obvious what would happen, him being a Hunter at a public high school. Zain nods his head, and a second later Rain does too. Once everybody has agreed, we all turn back to Alexander. "We accept," I say for all of us.

"Good, because I don't know what I would do if you declined. I suppose you still can, but, y'know. Alright I'm just gonna say it." He takes a deep breath and looks each of us in the eye. "The International Demon Hunting Society would like to officially recruit you to their team, to become Undercover Hunters- in-Training."

CHAPTER 6

"What?" I ask.

There's no way this is real. This Alexander guy has to be joking. There's no way.

"Yep," Alexander says. "Here's where that choice comes in. You can always say no to this responsibility and no one would hold it against you, but you'd have to have your memory wiped. Of course, if you said yes, you wouldn't be able to tell anyone about this, ever. There's also the matter of-"

"Why us?" Rain interrupts.

"That's a good question. The Council made a special exception for you four."

"The Council?" I mumble.

"They're this group of highly trained Hunters. That's all I can say."

This is almost too much for my brain to process. Hunters-In-Training? Just like that? Wasn't there a whole audition process or something? And wasn't it supposed to be really hard? But they just came to us? I'm not that in-the-know with IDHS, or Hunters, for that matter. Is this a normal thing they did? Grab kids from schools? Did this mean I just had to pick everything up and leave?   "So, how is this hypothetically going to work?"

The boy, who I found out from social media when I was at the shelves, is named Milo. "And why have us come up here and clean when you could have just told us first thing?"

"That was my sense of humor, I suppose," Alexander says. "Basically every day after school you will go to the IDHS building and train. Then, once you're fully there and prepared, you will be given your first assignment as a team. If you succeed, you will be full-blown Undercover Hunters. If you fail, you will keep trying until you succeed. I suppose I could tell you all of the fine print once we get there, though."

"Whoa wait hold on," the girl with dark skin intervened, who I also found out is named Stella. "Why did you come and get us? Isn't there a whole acceptance thing you have to do to new recruits? And where are we going to be going? How are we supposed to get there after school, anyway? This all makes no sense, like, at all."

"Well, the Council, once again. You'll find out where we're going once you get there. Though, of course, you still need to commit to this. If you tell anybody, and I mean anybody about this, we really will come for you. This isn't a joke. This isn't a one-and-done thing. This is, quite literally, life or death. With one little mistake, a person's life could end. If you don't think you're up for it, you don't have to do this. But, if you succeed and kill some demons, so many lives could be spared. Your life could be spared. Take as much time as you need to figure it out. For the sake of safety and federal reasons, I can't tell you anything more than that."

It was quiet for a while after that, everyone processing what he just said. I turn toward the group, whose faces are all slack-jawed. I fidget with the cuff of my sleeve. Everything seems unreal.

Like this is all just a dream. Of course, it isn't, but then I grasp something. If I really have to go to this mystery place every day after school, I can't have detention, which really throws a hole in the bet. Plus, my bank account. I could always stop the bet. Say I'd had enough of what the world had to offer or something. If this is really as important as Alexander makes it out to be, I kind of have to.

Milo is the first one to speak. "I'm in," he says. "I really don't like being home after school, plus it would be amazing to save some people."

"I'm in too," I say without really thinking. "I mean, it is for the greater good, right?"

"Uhm, this would kind of ruin our after school time, right?" Rain asks. "I'm not totally sure if I want this. I want to be with my family. Plus, I'm not sure my mom would believe me if I said I was hanging out with friends, because, well, I'm not all that popular."

"Yeah," Stella says. "Not sure about all of you, but I have a reputation to keep. I'm not totally sure if I want to be hanging out with... you guys, no offense. Plus, I have friends I need to talk with after school."

"Are you guys serious?" Milo snaps. "We have the chance to save people, save ourselves, help the world, maybe even become famous, and you want to turn that down for... high school social life?" He says the last words with a pointed look at Stella.   "Hey," Rain says. "I never said I wanted to turn this down, I just don't know how I'm going to convince my parents to let me go out if I'm not friends with anyone."

"Fine, I can help you with your problem," Milo says. "I can be your friend. You can hang out with me."

"Oh," Rain mumbles.

Milo nods.

"Ok-ay," Stella chimes in, saving everyone from that weird inter-action. "That solves her problem, but what about me? I still have friends outside of school. I still have friends in school. I can't just throw that away!"

"Yes, you can!" I shout. "This is stupid, we shouldn't be arguing about this. The answer is obvious, Stella! Look, I'll call off the bet right now so I don't have detention every day anymore. Watch." Pulling my phone out, I vigorously type a message.

From recent events, I've decided to call off the bet from here on out. I'm sorry to anyone who had plans to participate. Thank you for your understanding.

"Wow," Milo mumbles. "He actually did it. Why so formal?" Everyone, including Alexander, crowds around Milo to look at my screen.

"How else are they supposed to know I'm serious?" I put my phone back in my pocket. "Please, Stella. Fighting isn't going to make the decision any more obvious."

Stella, looking around at each face, sighs. "You guys are crazy." With that, she turns to the exit of the attic and starts walking toward it. I groan in annoyance. Stella just puts a foot down on the first step when she stops. She seems to think for a moment. She turns toward us again and locks eyes with me. Something in my gaze must have made Stella change her mind, because she takes a step away from the staircase and towards the group.

"Don't make me regret this." She crosses her arms over her chest and looks at Alexander.

"Alright, so I take it everyone has come to an agreement," Alexander says, crossing the room to an empty wall. "If you'll all please follow me over here." We do. He holds up his wrist, where a bracelet with a sparkling white crystal is. "This is the official IDHS bracelet. The public doesn't know about it because it could be incredibly dangerous. This bracelet is where all of your information is stored. It's a tracker, a communicator, a clearance key, and it's used as transportation." He then points to his neck, where a necklace with a matching white crystal is. "This is-"

"Woah, wait!" I interrupt. "Are we just gonna skip over the 'transportation' part? What do you mean by that?"

"In a minute," Alexander replies. "This is the IDHS necklace, and it helps us breathe where we're going. It also doubles as an extra tracker and-"

"Breathe?" Stella asks. "Can't we do that with, I don't know, our respiratory systems? Why do we need a choker to breathe for us? Also, why are these names so boring? Can't they be called-"

"In. A. Minute." Alexander repeats the words through gritted teeth. "It doubles as a tracker and a stylish clearance key, like your bracelet. Now back to the bracelets. When you use-"

"Why do we need so many tracker-"

"IN A MINUTE!" Alexander screams. We recoil as he smooths down his already-perfect hair. "What I mean when I say you can use your tracker for transportation, is that it can do this!" He holds up his wrist and taps a button I didn't see before. He makes a big clockwise circle with his arm, his hand fisted. When he gets back to the top position, he opens his hand and flicks his wrist. He looks back smugly.

To my shock, a small black circle starts to form in the middle of the circle he drew in the air. The black dot begins to spin, and it gets bigger, fading to a dark blue. Then a light blue at the edges. It's the exact size of the circle he made in the air. It swirls, making a strange, wind-like sound.

He had made a portal.

I'm the first to scramble back from it. I yelp in surprise. The others quickly follow suit, reacting milliseconds differently. Alexander laughs and walks up, right beside the portal.

"It really is harmless, guys," he says, sticking his arm into the middle. Awestruck, I slowly walk to the back of the portal. His hand is gone.

"Woah..." I mumble. I walk over to where Alexander is and stick my arm through like he did. I felt...nothing on the other side. No wind, sunlight, nothing. It didn't even feel like I had an arm. It was weird. I pull it back out quickly.

"Last chance to back out, everybody," Alexander says, looking at Stella. All she did was stare back. "Okay then, take a choker and a bracelet." He holds out his hand with many chokers and bracelets in it. We grab them and put them on. "Alright, go ahead and follow me. It'll feel weird, but it'll be worth it for the view you're about to get." He steps into the portal, having to put his foot in first, like he's getting in a car.

Milo is the next to go, stepping hesitantly into the portal like Alexander did. Gaping at the swirling blue portal, Rain goes next. I look at Stella, but she's looking down at the floor, shuffling her feet.

"Stella."

She looks up at me.

"You go next," I say, gesturing toward the portal. "I'm here for you."

Stella, rolling her eyes, steps forward. She goes up to the portal and is about to step through when she stops and looks at me. Her face is sincere. "Thank you."

"No problem."

With that, she steps into the portal. Then, she's gone. Taking a deep breath, I step in front of the swirling mass. This is it. No going back now. I hope I'm making the right choice as I step into oblivion.

The world around me twists and warps, making me want to vomit. It is cold and cruel in the void, yet at the same time there is no feeling. It felt like floating, but also flying straight forward at an alarming speed. Up is down. Left is right. Right is wrong. When it feels like it will never end, the portal spits me out in a place that was at the bottom of the list of what I expected.   Space.

CHAPTER 7

The planet we are standing on is very small compared to Earth and has a pale green color. Except, the sphere is cut in half, so it's only the bottom half of the said sphere. In the middle of everything is an incredibly beautiful, sparkling castle made out of what looks like crystal. A path leads toward the castle, the same path on which we are standing, but it also exits at many different points, leading all around the place. People of all different kinds are milling about and chatting.

I realize with a jolt that these people are Hunters. I even recognize some of them. There's the Aces, an all boy Group that was established a couple of years ago. The Apocalypse, a somewhat older Group that has been Hunting since I can remember. The last one around the academy is some people I don't recognize, so they were probably an Undercover Group.

The castle is surrounded by a moat, with four rivers flowing out toward the edges of the planet, right at each cardinal point. The streams, to my shock, flow right off the planet and into the abyss of space. There seems to be no shortage of water, though, as it keeps flowing. The most shocking part about any of it, though, is the sky. Or, moreso, the lack of it.

There are three planets floating in space. The first one is pink, with huge purple rings surrounding it. The surface is still, no storms or clouds. The second planet is a multi-colored one, with green, blue, and yellow splotches all over.

The surface has a few clouds, but none too crazy. The last planet is a deep red, like the surface of mars. All around us is inky black with stars speckled everywhere.

I know there's a sun in this solar system, but it's probably behind the other planets. Looking back at the planet I'm standing on, I see that it's completely artificial, with no atmosphere, and it isn't as big as the planets in the sky. Looking back at everyone's faces, and seeing they were just as shocked as I feel, I get reassured that this is absolutely insane.

"Welcome to Ecsporavet," Alexander says. "The land of the Hunters."

"So the theory was right," Milo whispers. "I was not expecting this."

Major understatement.

"Wait," Stella says. "How can we hear each other? Isn't space a vacuum?"

"Of course it is," Alexander replies. "Just another part of Megicusus."

"Megi what?" Zain asks.

Alexander holds up his wrist to the top of the circle and taps the button that started them off with his middle finger. The portal flashes out of sight. "I'll get to that." He starts walking toward the castle. We follow him. "Now I can explain to you everything we know so far. No more secrets, no more lies. It all started way back on May 25th, 2041, at one thirty-eight pm, when the Outbreak of the Underworld struck our world in Siberia. There's this crater there called the Batagaika crater, well, that's at least what they called it before the Outbreak.

Now they call it the no-man's land. It's in this mountain range that's not so cold anymore. Anyway, no one knows why all the demons and ghosts waited until then to come, especially if they've been around this whole time. That didn't matter to us back then. What mattered was when people started to get brutally murdered by these demons that came.

"We had no way of getting rid of them, so the military and government decided to go, trying to capture one of these things. Reports from soldiers who came back told that the locals said this crater seemed to get bigger each year until eventually it cracked open. We covered it with Calapimaentum later, but I'm getting ahead of myself.

When we finally got a hold of one tangible demon at the scene, one we later identified as a Reincarnated Ala demon, most of the soldiers sent were dead. Most of the civilians around the area, too. It was gorey and terrifying, but they got that creature out of there, and immediately sent it to the labs. The soldiers tried to bring everyone to safety. It was too late, though. Everybody in that surrounding city was killed, including the soldier team. The demon force, with nothing else in the city, started spreading around the area, going from town to town.

"While all this was going on, the scientists were scrambling to concoct something that could kill this Ala demon they got a hold of. Many brainstorming sessions later, they decided to get a sample from the opening in the crater, and that's how we got Megicusus. With the technology we had then, it took a while, but they got the thing duplicated within two hours.

Then, with the product, they mixed it with ingredients even I don't know, and tested it on the demon. It, thankfully, worked, and the demon was dead as soon as the mixture entered their bloodstream. We later named the substance Goph, and it kills demons as soon as it touches the blood in their system. We then replicated this on a widespread scale, and had special soldiers sent in from all over the world to get training on how to use Goph and inject it in the best way possible. You'll learn it soon at the Academy." He says the last sentence with a point at the castle, which we are currently heading toward.

"The world finally joined together, and we defeated the demons by a very close call. The other demons retreated, and the entire world scrambled to put a solution together. We eventually came up with IDHS, and the Public Barriers were put up with Megicusus. We found out that Megicusus could be used for many of the problems with demons, and we made Calapimaentum. We have very special teams that go out of the Public Barriers to seal any new openings found. IDHS, recently formed, put together many different people who wanted to help. Nowadays, we have a more formal way of doing it with the Council and the acceptance regiment, but we were desperate back then. We found out that almost anything could be done with Megicusus, so that's probably the solution to any questions you have about how it all works. We, of course, hid it from the public eye, in case it got into the wrong hands.

"Ghosts were an entirely different problem, because nothing could enter their bloodstreams. So we had to make a special device with Megicusus called a Phor that would help ghosts that didn't make it to the other side find their fate. They get judged by whatever being is up there. From there, they can either get accepted into heaven or thrown into the Underworld, and then we'll just have to deal with them all over again as a Reincarnated Demon. A never ending cycle"

"Wait," I say, finally interrupting his ramblings. We're now crossing a crystal bridge that looks straight out of a fairytale. "Can we please get a list of some sort of all the different types of demons? This is all getting confusing."

"Yeah, we have a list inside. Of demons, ghosts, and other creatures. You'll get it in no time."

Finally, we get to the Academy, as Alexander called it, and we enter through the tall, glittering doors. We are at the start of a very long hallway, with pictures of people scattered along the walls. "The school has six wings, the first four being Egyn, Oriens, Amaymon, and Paymon. The four cardinal directions, or regions in the Under- world. Each demon comes from one of these regions, and that region is where you will learn about each species. The tower in the middle of the campus is the fifth wing, or the Ghost wing, where you will learn about ghosts and other creatures. The last wing, the one we are in right now, is called the Training wing, where you will get weapons and train with them. It's also where we deploy our Hunters."

I make a map of everything in my head. The first place we get to, the gateway into Ecsporavet, is at the southeast bottom. The entrance to the Academy is also at the southeast, and the Training Wing is with the entrance. If her reasoning was correct, The Egyn wing is in the north, the Oriens is in the east, the Amaymon is in the south, and the Paymon is in the west. The rivers extend from the four main wings. Then the Ghost wing is in the middle of the island, and the Academy.

We continue on through the hall. The pictures on the walls are of people I don't know, they are all mostly old and wrinkly. There are a few chandeliers in the ceiling and the floor is a beautiful white. When we finally get to the end of the hallway, where a door identical to the one outside stands, Alexander stops.

"This is where the key part of your bracelets come in," he says, holding up his wrist to a small scanner by the door I didn't notice before. When the white stone meets the scanner, it makes a beeping noise and flashes a green light, startling me. The doors open up, revealing a large hall, where in the middle is a huge spiral staircase, going up. The people milling about range from anywhere between teens and adults, all chatting and reading and being normal-looking. A few groups I recognize, like the Vixens and the Crush, but some I don't. The room is the same crystal as the outside, except now there are doors and openings into gym-like rooms with devices and weapons lined up on the walls. People in the room, seeming to be suddenly aware of our presence, shift away from us, as if scared. Of what, I have no clue.

"This is the Training wing. Down here is just practicing and casual, plus the break room over there," he points to the general left direction, "but upstairs there are simulation tests that your group can use to climb the ranks and take on more advanced demons. Also in that middle floor is where groups set out to take care of assignments, but you'll learn more about that later. At the very top is the Council room, where they make important decisions about recruits and other things. There isn't really much in this wing that I can show you today, but I guess that's true for every wing. I'll show you the others."

He wanders toward the middle of the room, right before the staircase, and turns right, toward the Oriens wing doors, clearly marked with a green sign. To the left of the staircase is a door marked with a red Amaymon. We go into the Oriens wing behind him.   We enter a hallway identical to the last one, except instead of random people on the wall, it is of newspaper articles of IDHS. Dating back from 2040, when IDHS was first founded, all the way to the present. When we get to the end, Alexander does the same thing with the original doors, scanning the small stone on his wrist.

This wing is large like the other one, but with lots more rooms. The Training room's crystals were multi- colored, sort of like an opal. The Oriens wing's crystals, however, have a more green-ish color. There are banners of demons at each door, showing us what to expect. Most of the banners are repeated though, probably because there aren't many demons in the Oriens category. "The thing about each wing is that they are color-coded," Alexander informs us. "Green being the easiest demons to defeat, red being the hardest."

We keep walking, going through another door in front of us. The next hallway has nothing in it, no pictures or such, just a straight shot toward the Egyn wing. This wing has a yellow tint to it, sort of like if the sun were to be shining through the crystals. This wing is probably the second easiest, if the color scale follows the direction we are moving. The doors, once again, have little banners beside them featuring demons.

The next wing, Paymon, is basically an exact replica of Oriens' wing, but it has an orange tint. The hallway before, once again, has no decorations in it. I think that this is getting really repetitive, going around in a big circle, looking at the walls and colors. When we finally get to the last wing, the Amaymon wing, I'm not expecting much from it.

The crystals are a deep red tint, and there are banners of different demons by different doors, like any other wing, except the people wandering around are holding themselves straighter, as if scared of even the teachers seeing them unworthy. All of the people in this wing are people I do recognize, really professional groups that seem to be on Assignments all the time.

The last hallway has pictures of different Hunter Groups on the walls, some I recognize, some I don't, some Undercover. All diverse and unified. All smiling and proud of what they've accomplished. I have an overwhelming wave of longing. Wanting to be in a group like that. Then I realize, that group is around me. I had found my friends.

CHAPTER 8

"These are the sheets of demons and other creatures," Alexander says, handing each of us a packet of papers. We are standing in the training room, beside the main doors. "You can look at it later tonight, but for now, it's time for you to go home. Get a good night's rest, go to school tomorrow, then come right back here. I'd recommend coming together in a place you won't be noticed leaving or coming back. When you make a portal back to Earth, you have to think of the place you want to go to, so I think you guys should go back to the school's attic. In order to leave and come back, just do the motion that I did when I first got you here. Good night and good luck."

With that, we step outside. We walk toward the entrance, Zain speaking first. "I think we need a name for our group. It feels awkward just calling us 'that one group'. Anyone have any ideas?"

"Okay, first things first," Stella says. "We need everyone's names." One by one, we all say our first and last names. Everyone has a small shock when Zain says Z, even though that is technically what he prefers to be called.

"I think we need more time to think, right?" I suggest. "We probably need the group name to be based on our names so it's easy to remember, right?"

"Understandable," Z says, finally reaching where the portal spat them out. "So, how does this work again?" Z holds up his wrist, flicking it and then spinning in a circle.

"Where'd you even get that?" Rain asks, holding up her wrist and copying the motion Alexander had made perfectly. The portal swirls and shows up. "I'll go last so I can close it."

Z goes first, falling backwards into the portal with a whoop. He disappears and Stella steps up next, hopping into it with grace. Then it's my turn. I wave to Rain and step into the portal. A smile spreads over my face as I speed through time and space, even though I don't know what I'm doing and it doesn't make sense. Then, I get shot out and land in a crouch, just in front of the portal. I straighten up and step to the side just as Rain goes through. Knowing she isn't going to land upright, I speed toward her and catch her just before she descends to the ground.

I straighten her up and step away quickly. I told myself I would do it for anyone. I look at Rain and see she is blushing. Instead of saying thank you, she holds up her wrist, presses the button, and flicks her hand down. All at once, the portal falls away, disappearing from the space just as quickly as it appeared. I look at the whole group, Z and Stella closer to the exit of the attic.

"Well, see you guys tomorrow at school?" Z asks, gesturing toward the exit, where the stairs are still down.

"See you then," Stella monotones, stepping down the stairs. Z follows her down, then Rain right after her.

"Wait," I call. "Where do we meet after school?"

"We could meet...by the water fountains?" Rain suggests, her hair bouncing as she nods. "That way we could seem inconspicuous."

"Sure," Z says from down the stairs.

"Do some studying tonight too!" I shout after them.

One by one, we go down the stairs, each heading in different directions at the bottom. I go toward the stairs going down to the floor level. I walk the halls, pondering everything that has been said to me, trying to piece some things together. In barely an hour, I had gone into space, been accepted as a hunter-in-training, and learned that portals were real and that I could make one at any given moment in time.

Whoa.

Whatever doubts I had about what was happening to me being fake vanished away. This was real. What was I getting myself into? Something terrifying, that's for sure. I get to the front door of the school. Looking to my right at the bike racks, I see that mine is one of the only ones there, locked up with a chain. Pulling out my key from my pocket, I unlock the bike, stowing away my key once again. I pull it out of the rack and hop on, speeding away into the road.

My house is pretty far away from the school, in an entirely different Public Barrier. I ride off quickly, wanting to get home soon before my parents. I get to the transport rails and ride up the ramp going to the stations. The rails rise up above the ground outside the Public Barriers, sort of like an old train, with mini Barriers around each car. The cars are usually occupied with two or three people.

I hop off my bike and walk into the line, marked clearly with 'Public Barrier Two of Pittsburgh', and I impatiently tap my foot behind the person in front of me. When it's finally my turn, I hop onto the train car and sit quickly, leaning my bike up against the wall. Two others come in, an older woman and a middle aged man, and they sit in different chairs around the car. The door slides shut, and a mini Barrier pops up around the car. The car goes up the rails and stops before the Public Barrier. A space the size of the Mini Barrier opens in the Public Barrier and the car zooms through fast, the space closing right behind them. As they ride past, I notice that beneath us, through the window, a few openings into the Underworld are sealed with Calapimaentum, but there are two or three demons wandering around, not yet taken care of by the Hunters. They probably look longingly up at the car as we drive past. They were too far away to see any distinguishable features, but I just know. I hate demons.

A shiver goes down my spine and I look away, instead staring up at the approaching Public Barrier. This Public Barrier is where most of the rich people in the city of Pittsburgh are at. I always wonder why my parents don't just take me to a private school that is closer to home, they certainly have the money for it. Maybe it's so that I can learn what other kids' lives are like. If that was it, that plan was terrible. Today's group was the first 'friends' I had ever had.

The area we're riding over apparently used to be a river, but I have a hard time picturing that. There's an old, deteriorating bridge we ride over, following its path from multiple decades before. I think about the people that lived here years before, where they like me?

The car finally gets to the Public Barrier, the small hole opening quickly, and the car going even faster, flying through the opening and closing just as quickly as it had opened. The car skids to a stop and the Mini Barrier falls away. The door opens. I pull my bike out of the car and hop on it as soon as I can, swerving around people milling around.

I ride down the ramp, picking up speed and zooming down the roads. I pass by many big houses before I finally pull up onto my street. I speed up, zooming by multiple houses before I finally see mine in the distance. No cars are in the driveway, but they could be in the garage. I cycle like a maniac up to my house, swerving into the driveway. I skid to a stop by the garage, hop off my bike, and open the garage door.

Both of my parents' cars are there. Cursing, I put my bike up against the left wall, then walk toward the door. I nudge it open, glad nobody is waiting for me. Maybe they didn't notice I was gone. It wouldn't surprise me. I creep around the corner, and with nobody there in the large house, I tip-toe to the staircase and start creeping up. I get to the second floor without a hitch, but my room is on the third floor, and I can't risk taking the elevator when it's so loud. I proceed up the stairs, avoiding all the spots that creak, though there are very few. It seems like years before I finally make it to the third floor, but when I do, my heart stops.

My parents are there, staring at me, like they were waiting. They probably were. My dad's black hair shines in the sun, his brown eyes roving me up and down. My mom's blackish brown curly hair flows down her shoulders, her dark eyes glaring at me.

"Hi," I say, crossing my arms.

"Would you like to explain to us why you're late?" my mom asks, staring down her nose at me.

"You know the answer to that," I say, shifting my bag on my shoulders.

"Yes, we do," my dad responds. "We just want to hear it out of your mouth."

Making an annoyed noise, I finally mumble: "I got detention."

"Disgraceful," my mother says, turning away. "You get a week of grounding."

"What?" I blurt. "You can't do that!"

"Yes, we can," my father says. "I'm tired of your attitude and it's time you learn your place in this household. You are the child. You are nothing but a child. We are the parents, and you will learn to respect us. Now go to your room. I expect you at dinner at six-thirty."

My mouth hangs open. First week at a job and I'm already losing it. Just my luck. I stomp away toward my room, slamming my door and flopping onto my bed, throwing my bag down too. I lay there, looking up at the ceiling for a while. I know that if I started crying I wouldn't be able to stop, so I keep it bottled up. Then, suddenly remembering the papers we all got, I snatch my bag up and unzip it, pulling out the paper as I unfold it quickly.

Demon types

Reincarnated-The most common demon type, occurs to all demons except for the Amaymon. They seemed to be human in their past lives.

Pure-The demons from the original group that were first put into the Underworld. They are older than time and are nearly impossible to kill. Only occurs to Amaymon creatures.

Demons

Oriens

Imp- A small, annoying creature that doesn't do a lot of damage, a prankster of sorts. It's very mischievous and can be easily killed. It can fly and looks like a gremlin with wings. Some can even turn invisible.

Shedim- A gray, tall creature with an arched back and short front arms. It has a long tail and spikes along its back. Also has sharp teeth and a very long tongue. Not always evil, sometimes even helpful to humans, though by law, we still have to kill them. They usually willingly oblige.

Ghoul- Looks a lot like a gray zombie, sometimes even ghosts. The demon version of ghouls are easy to kill, but are still dangerous. They are mostly found at graveyards, feeding on dead flesh.

Egyn

Ravener- Gray, humanoid creature whose mouth opens incredibly wide, some even taking on a worm bottom half. These creatures are mindless and will try to kill anything that moves, but they're somewhat slow and easy to kill.

Achaierai- Creatures that stand like a human but have goat limbs and hair. They have no eyes and rely on their sense of smell and hearing. They have long horns with long tongues.

Naga- Serpent-like creatures, sometimes with a humanoid torso. They come in blue, green, and red, and they can sometimes be found with spears or whips.

Croucher- A tan humanoid with long horns. It has a patch of black hair in the back of its head that grows long. The demon, despite eating a lot, is very skinny.It has long claws and sharp teeth.

Hellhound- A terrifying dog that is made of bones. It's always on fire and never seems to be put out. Some dogs can grow more than one head, like the famous Cerberus.

Paymon

Ala-Demon with four yellow eyes that has horns. It has very long limbs and odd, shredded wings that somehow keep it upright. This demon can also control the weather,making it storm or wind.

Amphisbaena- A snake with a bird body, having snake necks and heads popping out of each end. The creature is very difficult to kill, having to first amputate both heads before injecting it with Goph.

Cherufe- Stone beasts with four legs that travel like a lion. It's a lava creature, controlling it and fire to their command.

Amaymon

Cecaelia- Water demons with a human body and eight tentacles where their legs should be. They are cunning and incredibly hard to kill under the water, which is why they are put into the Paymon category.

Shax- A commander of over 30 legions in the Underworld. He has a stork-like body that's as tall as a human's. He usually wears a black robe. He has the power to take away any sense of understanding and has evil horses for each legion.

The seven Princes of the Underworld- not much is known about them, only that they run most of everything and are what some would call "the seven deadly sins".

(Not all of the Amaymon demons have been recorded)

Ghosts

Yurei-A ghost that doesn't have a distinct reason for still wandering, they just do. They're sometimes dangerous, but it depends.

Banshee- A ghost that can take on appearances and voices of loved ones, causing people to go straight into the face of danger without thinking.

Onryo- A ghost that was once abused by a lover, very vengeful ghosts that will attack anyone except for their past love. Catch with a Phor.

Ubume- Ghost parents that will care for their past children with small miracles. Catch with a Phor.

Goryo- Very dangerous ghosts that were murdered in their past life and still hold somewhat of a grudge. Catch with a Phor.

Funayurei- Ghost that died with relation to water. Somewhat dangerous, can control water. Catch with a Phor.

Zashiki- Children ghosts with a playful spirit. Not very danger-ous. Catch with a Phor.

Kodama- Ghosts that inhabit trees, child-like bodies with black holes where their eyes and mouth are. Catch with a Phor.

(Keep in mind that ghosts are just lost spirits, they don't mean to cause harm)

Other Creatures

Chupacabra- A creature with the wings and ears of a bat but the body of a starving dog. It will eat most animals and humans. Many people mistake the Chupacabra with a demon even though it's considered a creature. Can only kill it by beheading because it can regenerate its flesh and limbs.

Vampires- A human-like creature that sucks the blood of oth-ers, a vampire bite can kill you contrary to belief of it turning you into one of its kind. Despite being romanticized in films and books this creature is very dangerous.

Werewolves- Only come out at night, usually humans who turn and can't regain their memory of what they did while in the wolf form. There is usually a cure for werewolves so try to have them make it until the morning so we can treat them.

Cyclops- A very strong, tall humanoid creature with one eye. Very thick skin so you have to dig deep to kill.

Siren- A beautiful creature representing what looks like a mer-maid. Lives in salt waters. Lures people with songs and kills them. Don't be fooled by their song, anyone can fall in love with them.

Hydra- A horse made out of water. They try to drown you in the water. The only way to kill them is with a special machine called a Hyphix.

Kappa- A duck-like creature that's green with a bowl of water on its head that gives it power. Drain the water bowl to kill it. The

Kappa is found in water, is as tall as a human, and will try to drown you.

Kitsune- A fox creature that can shapeshift into any form. Hard to spot, not that hard to kill. Stab it once and it should die.

Too exhausted and angry to memorize it, I throw it on my desk and check my phone. It's almost six-thirty. Groaning, I stand up and throw open the door, storming down the hall.

CHAPTER 9

I throw open the door to my house, dropping my bag by the door. I hear my golden retriever, Beanie, pad down the hall. When she sees me, she barks and runs up to my knees. I kneel down and pat the dog, closing the door behind me. Sighing, I stand up and step around her, walking down the hallway with my shoulders slumped. Walking into the living room, I see my dad sitting on the couch. My spirits instantly brighten.

"Dad!" I shout. I run up to him and tackle him in a bear hug. My dad, pulling away, studies my face, his brown eyes growing wide as he seems to remember something. He pulls away, readjusts his shirt, then frowns at me.

"You got detention today?" dad asks.

"Oh, that," I say. "The teacher gave me detention because I got one push up less. That's the stupidest thing ever. Coach has no clue what a punishment is."

"Nonetheless," dad scolds, "you should never get in trouble with teachers. I thought you knew better."

"Also," my mom interrupts, coming into the room. "You missed dad coming home. If you don't wanna miss anything else, you really shouldn't be getting detention."

"I guess that's true," I mumble. Then I remember that I most definitely will be missing more chances to see my family, with me now having to go to Ecsporavet every day after school, and my mood dips again. "Also, can I go out after school tomorrow? I want to hang out with my friends."

Mom blinks. "Uhm, sure. Just don't be surprised if we get ice cream without you."

"No worries," I say, "I'm not all that concerned. When's dinner going to be ready?"

"Right now, actually," mom says, walking over to the oven. "It's lasagna! Your favorite!"

I smile. Mom dishes out plates to each of us, sitting down at the couch in the living room. Dad turns on the TV to Jeopardy, us guessing the answers, not always correctly, every time in between mouthfuls. Beanie eating her food too in the corner by the TV.

After that I wander up to my room and shower, standing under the hot, running water for a while, contemplating everything. I know it's childish, but I feel somewhat giddy with the fact that I can have friends, real friends, if I didn't mess this up.

I was, probably, going to mess it up.

Now, laying on my bed, I stare at my phone. Sure enough, there's Z's post. No explanation. Just a small sentence. And a lot of comments and likes. I sigh and decide to look up the others in the group. Stella's a popular girl at school, but she's never really mean to anybody. Her follower count is somewhat high, based on how many people are in the school. She has a lot of posts, pictures of friends, memes, whatever. I then look up Milo. He has a handful of followers, no posts.

I scroll around for a while, then put my phone face down on the bed. I then dig around in my bag and pull out the packet Alexander gave us, staring at it with my brow furrowed. I give up and just decide to put it away in my desk. I run through a list of school assignments in my head and, deciding I have nothing to do, pull out my book from my bag and start reading it.

I've always loved reading. It let me go to a new world, one where I didn't have to deal with anything. I, of course, have a decent life. I have somewhat-good grades, a loving family, and a super cute dog. I've never had any friends, though, and I'm very introverted. I realize, suddenly, that maybe I do have friends now. I know that's wishful thinking, though, and I smother the thought before it can spread.

With a sigh, I put my book away, lay back down on my bed, and shut my eyes, trying to get my head to calm down. I drift off to sleep.

Chapter 10

I wake up and rub the sleep out of my eyes. I had barely slept at all last night, my mind running with questions and ideas. I grab an outfit out of my closet, a white crop top with a red jacket and cargo pants. I go to the bathroom and get ready, doing simple makeup with my hair down, showing off my afro curls.

I walk down the steps, seeing my mom setting out breakfast at the table. My dad had died when I was five, and ever since my mom has been the best at providing for both of us to live comfortably with her stay-at-home teaching job. She never cared if I got in trouble, just always told me to not lose hope. I never know what to not lose hope on, but I always take the advice to heart. I wonder, sometimes, if maybe she's saying the advice to herself as much as she is to me. I plop down on the chair and start eating off my plate.

"Hey, mama," I greet.

"Morning, Starshine," she sits next to me with her own plate of food. "How'd you sleep?"

"Fine."

I start running through a list of questions I would discuss with my new friends. I know I shouldn't be harsh, but I just can't get over it. I refuse to sit at their table today, I would sit with my real friends and show them what they mean to me. They helped me out through a lot of tough times. I would do the same for them, even if I would be living a double life.

As my mind goes through what was and wasn't acceptable for my life now, I realize I should have left for school a few minutes ago. "Oh! I got to go, mama." I shoot out of my chair and give mom a quick hug, pull my converse on my feet and grab my bag as I run out the door.

I hop on my bike and ride toward the school. I don't care if I'm late, I just really don't want to get detention. I also want to explain to Elsie what had happened, leaving out a few details, of course, but the gist of it. As I approach the building I see Elsie by the door, obviously waiting for me. I hop off my bike and put it in the bike rack, locking it up and shoving the key in my pocket. Elsie spots me and waves. I head toward her.

"What on Earth, Stella!" Elsie shouts. "One minute we're skipping class, the next this guard comes in and takes you, without taking me, and when I ask about it, all you tell me is 'I have no clue what's going on'. Real discreet, Stella. Then, on top of all that, you don't answer my texts all night. All night! Seriously! You scared the ever-living hell out of me! Gah, I can't believe you! You better start talking!"

"Look, all that detention teacher did was make us clean a dusty old attic. I forgot what his name was, he was so boring. After that I went home and slept because cleaning a big attic takes a lot out of you. Thanks for caring, though."

"That's it?" Elsie says, tapping her foot against the ground. "Well, then. Guess I was just worked up over nothing." She looks at me for a second, an odd expression on her face. Then, she walks inside the school, heading toward the locker bay. In a rush of brown hair, Livy joins our group. She's tall and has a gray hoodie on with ripped jeans. Livy, despite all her boring outfits, is really pretty. There's something about her that draws everyone's eyes.

"Hey, Elsie!" she greets her. Then, just acknowledging me, turns and smiles. She steps beside Elsie and starts rambling toward her, Elsie nodding and laughing. They walk to their lockers and open them up, right beside each other. My locker is in a whole other area, so I say goodbye and head toward my bay.

I'm just gathering the last of my books and closing the locker when Z appears beside me. I shut my locker and look at him.

"Hey," he says. "I've got a question." Everybody in the hallway is glancing at us, whispering. "Why do you think everyone's watching me?"

I shrug. "Oh, I don't know, maybe because you cancelled the bet that had the whole school in shambles trying to get money from you."

"Well, either way, I think we should talk about this whole thing at lunch. I already got Milo on board, now I just have to convince you and Rain. Should be easy to-"

"No," I interrupt.

He pauses. "What?"

"No. I'm not gonna sit with you guys at lunch. I have other friends, you know."

"Seriously? You're gonna reject us just because you have a few lousy friends that definitely don't deserve you?"

"Don't say that about them," I snap. "You barely even know them. If anything I don't deserve them. I'm not going to sit at lunch with you, but text me where we're going to meet after school. My number is on my profile. Goodbye."

I brush past him and head toward my first class, algebra, angry at his ego. How could he say that about people he hasn't even met? Mostly, though, I'm mad at myself for thinking a boy could be decent.

CHAPTER 11

I walk into the lunchroom and get my tray in line. I head over to the table I had told them all to come to. Rain and Milo are already there, sitting across from each other at the end of the table closest to the exit. They are having a hushed conversation, probably not wanting anybody to hear. I slide my tray next to Milo's and plop down in the chair. I look at them, and they both turn toward me.

"Where's Stella?" Rain asks.

I nod toward the table of popular kids. Sure enough, Stella's on the outskirts, like she's in on the conversation, but also isn't. "Hanging out with her 'friends.' Seriously, when is she gonna figure out that they're using her? It's obvious, this girl is seriously clueless."

"Well, takes one to know one," Milo says, gesturing toward Xavier, talking with his table and not once glancing at me.

"The thing about being the awesome person that is me is that you don't really have a close group of friends. Just sort of buddy-buddy with everyone. And I will take that as a compliment, loner."

"Hey," Milo retorts. "At least I like to be alone."

"Can we please focus?" Rain cuts in.

"Yeah," Milo says. "Where should we meet up? I vote for the alley just outside the school. No one ever goes in there, plus I found this little area down there where I go quite a bit."

"Alright, but how do we tell Stella where it is?" I ask. "She told me to text her when we find out what the meeting place is."

"Tell her to meet us at the water fountains at three-forty-five. Then I can take all of us there."

I pull out my phone and start looking for her profile online. Sure enough, there her phone number is. That's probably a privacy issue, I'll have to tell her to change that. I put her number in my phone and text her just what Milo told me to.

"I have a few questions for Alexander," Rain says through a bite of her food. She swallows, with a sour look on her face, and then keeps talking. "I'm confused on how we all got detention at the same time. It doesn't really make sense. It can't just be a coincidence, right?"

"That's a good question," I say, putting my phone away. "I guess I never really thought of it. Also, why so late, Milo?"

"What?"

"You said three-forty-five. School ends at three. Why so late?"

"I got grounded, so I have to go home then sneak back out again."

"Oh, that sucks," I take a drink of my milk. "Your parents strict?"

"Very."

"Well, guess you just have to fake it for them, too. Pretend you're in your room, then sneak out and come to IDHS. Like, all the time, though."

"Yeah."

"Guys, can we please focus?" Rain snaps. "We have to think of ideas to ask Alexander, not each other."

"You just have a great attitude, don't you?" I place my chin in my hand and look at Rain. "Like a little ray of sunshine." He snaps his fingers. "That's what I'm going to call you. Sunshine. Get it, 'cause your name is actually Rain?" I laugh like it's the funniest joke in the world.

"Unbelievable," Rain groans. She braces her arms on the table and leans forward a bit.

"Well, what about the fact that the teachers seemed extra cautious? It's like they were purposefully watching us." Milo takes a bite out of his food, some mystery soup the lunch staff made, and promptly puts it back down again.

"Yeah, the teachers did keep looking at me, but I thought it was just common practice, you know? Because I'm being sent to the office every other day," I add.

"I didn't notice anything different, except that my gym teacher is a snob." Rain scoffs. "Seriously, detention because I wasn't good at something? Sometimes I don't know about school staff. They suck."

"Okay, so one question we're going to ask is why the teachers were so observant. Anything else?" Milo rests his chin on his fist.

"Maybe," I provide. We sit in silence for a while and think. Alexander obviously didn't explain everything yesterday, but we're going to get more information today. Probably.

Suddenly Rain sits up straighter. "What about all those creatures on the list?" she taps her finger on the table. "I didn't know vampires and werewolves and sirens existed. I thought they were myths!"

"Same," Milo mumbles. "But we shouldn't be surprised any more. If I take one more piece of insane information my mind is literally going to implode. Like, seriously, I bet nobody in this school has gone to space before except for us. I almost passed out from panic up there."

"Yeah but I also bet nobody except for us are Hunters!" I exclaim. "I still don't quite believe it."

"Keep it down," Milo nudges me.

"What if it isn't real?" Rain asks suddenly. "What if it's a prank or something?"

"Rain, what are you talking about?" Milo questions. "Of course it's real." A pause. "Right?"

"Yeah, Sunshine over here is just getting philosophical on us." Z ruffles her hair from across the table. "Right, Sunshine?"

Suddenly the bell rings. We stand up and wait in line for the tray dump, silence falling over us like a blanket as we think. We go down the halls to the lockers where we go our separate ways. I'm looking at my feet as I walk and don't notice Stella standing in the way until I run into her.

I gasp a startled "Oof!" as her books and papers fall to the ground. I mumble a quick apology and gather up her books that fell from her hands. Stella is glaring at me when I straighten back up and hand over her things.

"Sorry," I say again, shrugging. "Did you get my text?"

Stella's mouth opens slightly. "Are you kidding me? Could you be any more inconsiderate? I'm so mad at you right now and you just shrug it off? Honestly, Z, I expected a lot more from you. I don't know why because you've done nothing to prove it to me, but can you blame me for hoping?"

I stare at her for a second, confused. What is she talking about? "What did I do?"

"Well, for one, you insulted me and my friends, which I don't like at all. Plus, you got my books dirty, so there's that too." She seems to realize how ridiculous this sounds because she blushes.

"I'm so, so sorry, princess. Would you like me to clean off your books and papers for you? How about I just clean your clothes too?" My voice turns so sarcastic it's monotone. "Oh, and let me just polish the ground before you step where other people's dirty-"

"Okay, I get it!" she shouts, stomping her foot. "Whatever." She storms off.

"Don't forget to check your phone!" I shout after her.

Instead of going to my locker, which I probably should have done for my stuff, I go to my next class, Precalc, and walk to my assigned spot. As I do, now becoming a pattern, a few people stop and stare at me, probably remembering the message online. I had to deal with this all day, people making sure it's real. Most of today somebody would do something and wait for me to make a move. I never did, though. I promised I wouldn't get detention, so I wouldn't get it.

Another one of my 'friends' comes in and sits beside me in their assigned spot. Jay takes out his notebook and opens it, glancing in Z's direction. "Did you really call off the bet?"

I sigh. "Yep."

"Oh."

'Oh' is right.

I was still kind of unsure as to why I would promise to not do the thing that was basically my whole personality. Thinking about it, I think I should look into getting a better hobby, or at least develop some other thing that was my thing. Instead of dwelling on it any longer, I grab a pencil from my bag and start twirling it in my fingers, letting the movement dull my thoughts.

CHAPTER 12

I'm by the water fountain, somehow the first one there despite having to go back to my house to make sure my parents knew I was 'home'. All went smoothly on that part, I think. When I got home, I stomped up to my room so that my parents knew I was there, and so that they knew I was mad. I locked myself in my room and put pillows in place under the covers so it would look like I was sleeping if they came in. It most likely wouldn't work so I was stuck hoping they wouldn't check on me or try to wake me up for dinner. Then I opened up the window as quietly as I could and put my athleticism to use.

I have taken karate since I could remember, because for one, my parents didn't like breaking traditions, and they did not like fighting, so that meant that it was my favorite thing to do. Another reason is because I don't like feeling weak. If I can't do something perfectly, I keep trying until I can, which is exactly why I have perfect grades.

I jumped out the window, rolling when I hit the ground to avoid getting hurt. It wasn't the most effective method of being silent, but I rode away with my bike quick enough that I was sure my parents didn't notice me.

Rain walks down the hall toward me, breaking my train of thought, and stopping to my right and looking around the area. She leans against the wall and crosses her arms over her chest. I watch her carefully. There's something about her today that radiates nonchalance, but another part of her screams hostility. I lean against the wall next to her, my features a slight smirk.

"Hey," I say.

Rain turns to me with a strange look on her face, bordering confusion and surprise. She turns her face away again. "Hi."

"So." I shift uncomfortably.

"So." Rain repeats.

"It's almost time for our first day, are you excited?" I ask.

She smiles. "Yep."

It's silent, a comfortable silence that I actually like. Z suddenly shows up and waltzes over to the water fountain. He waves and leans against the wall to my left.

"What's up, guys?" he asks, crossing one of his ankles over the other.

"Not much. Just waiting." Rain turns to him. "Where's Stella?"

"I'm sure she'll show up," he says. "Eventually."

We wait five more minutes, watching kids mill out of the front doors slowly. When Stella finally shows up, with an unamused look on her face, mostly every kid is gone. She stops in front of our trio and crosses her arms.

"Let's go," I say as I push off the wall. The group follows me at a steady pace, everyone keeping a few feet of space between each other. We exit the building and I walk down the streets into town. I go down the path I have gone down many times before. A right after two blocks, another right after three, a left after five, and finally a right just outside of Cindy's Peanut shop. The little alley was where my fondest childhood memories were. I stumbled upon it one day when I was ten after my dad made me stay outside all day for back-talking. I had spent the next seven years of my life there, doodling in my notebook, playing, imagining different things, sometimes just sitting in silence. I would climb up the ladder and sit on top of the tall peanut shop, letting the smell of it lull me into a sense of safety.

The back left corner of the alley had a tiny corridor to a small space where a rotting, abandoned cardboard box and a few rats were at. I deemed that my space and shooed the rats out to find a different home. Then I found an abandoned chair and a small coffee table that was broken in the dumpster. I somehow got them in through the tiny corridor.

Now, standing in the small space with my group, the furniture seems pathetic. Without dwelling on it too long, I squeeze toward the back wall and tap the button with my middle finger, making a large circle with my fist in the clockwise direction, opening it back up at the top and flicking my wrist. The blue portal swirls against the back wall. Without a word, I step through, getting sucked in.

I'm still not prepared for the ultra-confusing journey through time and space, but when I get back out onto Ecsporavet, I'm still not convinced it's real. I feel vomit in my throat but I swallow it back down. I step back from the entrance just as Rain warps back into reality where I was just standing. Her legs buckle but I catch her, setting her back upright again.

"Looks like you can't stop falling for me," I say, grinning. She turns pink and rolls her eyes, stepping away from me. Stella and Z appear, both almost falling, and I catch them both. Seems I'm the only one with balance in the group.

We go toward the entrance of the Academy. A few more groups have noticed us by now, staring obviously as we walk. A few people downright stop what they are doing and turn toward us. I take the liberty of quickening our steps toward the entrance.

We enter the doors and immediately see Alexander flirting with a tall blonde girl. He isn't very good at it. The girl has an unamused expression on her face as she walks off without saying goodbye.

"Smooth operator," Z muses as he slides up beside him. "I think she might just file a restraining order against you! Isn't that romantic?"

"Shut up," Alexander grumbles as he walks to the middle of the room where a desk with multiple pieces of paper on the surface is sitting. He picks the stack up and starts flipping through it. "Anyway, I've given you all time to think about everything that has been said to you. Since you guys start training today and you only have three hours before you have to get home, any questions? Please make them quick."

"Okay, we've all been thinking about it," I take hold of the situation. "We were wondering how the staff knew it was us getting detention? They seemed to be keeping a bigger watch on us than usual. Plus, how did we all get the same detention class when there's at least a few more classes."

Alexander smiles. "We may or may not have given an anonymous tip to the teachers about you four and how you were up to something that day. As for the detention class, I volunteered to take all the students. You four were fortunately the only ones that day. If there would have been other kids I would have let them off the hook early. Scheming is my favorite part of this job. Anyway, anything else?"

"Yes," Rain stands up taller. "I wanted to ask you, monsters are real? And I don't mean demons and ghosts, I mean Vampires and Werewolves. Let me guess, the next thing you tell us is that the Loch Ness Monster is real?"

"Actually, yes, but Nessie's species are human-eating monsters that can only come out at night, much like a Werewolf. That's why so many people are missing from that area."

If Rain's mouth can drop further it would be on the floor.

"Kidding." He finally finds the paper in the middle of the stack. "Nessie's actually really sweet, like a big underwater dog. She's the only one of her kind, sadly. We've been trying to help her, but she's pretty slippery. Anything else?"

Stella looks Alexander square in the eyes. "Well, if you know all about the afterlife and that paranormal, what religion is the real one?"

Religion is a touchy subject these days. Some of them are obviously out of the question based on demons and underworld stuff, but that didn't stop people from believing them anyway. I don't believe in Buddhism like my family does, but then again, I don't believe in any religion. I know there's a god up there because he's obviously judging where people go after death, but I believe if you did good, you could get in.

"We don't know," Alexander says. "Let people believe what they want. Science goes off the facts, and that's it. Now there's obviously some divine creature up there but we don't know the facts. It's all up to fate, chance, whatever you want to call it."

"Speaking of fate," Stella speaks up again. "Why? Why us? It doesn't make sense, what about everyone else?"

"Like I said before, it's up to the Councilors. They just know. They specifically asked for you guys. Don't ask me why again, if it were up to me you guys would probably be my last choice of candidates."

"Rude," Z grumbles.

"Whatever, here's your schedule. The first hour and a half will be learning about the Imps in Oriens for now. Then the rest of the time is yours to train and work out. Use it wisely, you guys will get your first assignment soon. Good luck." With that, he walks off.

"Okay..." Z looks at the paper. "Looks like we're going to the Imp classroom. Did you guys do the homework or was I not the only one who didn't look at the paper?"

"I did," Rain says, "but I didn't really go that in depth."

"Me neither," Stella mumbles.

"Unbelievable," I moan. "Am I the only one who cares?"

"No, we care!" Z snaps. "We just... don't care enough, I guess. It's fine though, they'll probably go over all of that boring stuff."

"It's not boring, it's very important to how we approach demons, ghosts, and other creatures. We can't just waltz in there and expect everything to go smoothly. Now come on, I'm not being in a team of people who don't know what they're doing."

"Speaking of which, what should our team name be?" Z taps his finger against his chin. "I was thinking of an abbreviation that only we know what it means, but what?"

"Maybe 'CG Team'," Rain says. "Because our 'leader' is 'Captain Grump'."

"Eh, I like the idea but it doesn't really roll off the tongue, y'know?" His brow furrows.

"What about something with 'Teen' in it?" Rain suggests again.

"I like that," Z says. "But what else are we? We could have a main gimmick we use or something. This is harder than I thought it would be."

"Who cares?" Stella grumbles. "Can we just go to our class?"

"No," Z retorts. "I'm not going until we get a name."

I sigh heavily. "If I give you a suggestion, can we please go to class?"

Z nods enthusiastically.

"Fine," I say. "What about 'TU Crew'? Stands for 'Teens Under-cover', because we're teens undercover?"

"Wow," Z mumbles. "That's actually really good. Who knew Captain Grump had it in him. Okay, guess we owe it to him to go to class or whatever."

We find the room quickly and find our seats inside. Two other teenagers are there, a girl and a boy. The girl is Asian like Milo, with long black hair pulled into a half-up half-down style. She has on a light blue t-shirt, sweatpants, and two different silver necklaces. There's a doodled smiley face on her arm and she's blowing a bubble from her gum. Her brown eyes skip over to us.

The boy has Almond brown skin and is sporting a beige shirt with white stripes and a pair of jeans. He has on heart sunglasses with gold trim and has dark brown, messy hair. His eyes are closed. On his head were headphones and he was nodding his head to music.

"Hey," the girl says. She's sitting to the right of me in the back of the two-by-three rows.

"Hello," I reply, looking around for the teacher.

"Are you going to ask me my name?" she asks.

My lips quirk at the edges. "Alright, what's your name?"

"Mikaya." Her nose crinkles. "Not Mikayla. Mikaya. No L."

"Ok, Mikaya no L, I'm Milo."

The girl's mouth drops. "Milo? As in Milo Milo?"

"Actually, my last name's Maeda."

The girl's jaw somehow drops lower. "No way..." She turns to the boy in front of her and smacks him on the shoulder. "Ro!"

The boy turns around. "Huh?" He pulls his headphones off.

"This kid's Milo Maeda!" she practically screams it.

"What!?" he blurts. He turns his disbelieving eyes to me and gives me a once over. "He's scrawnier than I expected.""Excuse you but I am a black belt in Karate," I cross my arms. "Besides, how and why do you know who I am?"

"Everybody knows who you are. Let me guess, she's Stella Booker?" Ro points to Rain, who's sitting beside him. Rain, who's been listening to this interaction, turns her unamused eyes over to him.

"No, that's Rain." I point to Stella, who's right in front of Rain. "That's Stella. Oh, and that's Z." I point to Z, sitting to the right of Stella. They turn at the sound of their names.

"You're telling me that the team with the most Future Fate is in the Imp class?" Ro laughs.

"Hey, that's rude, Ro," Mikaya says, smacking him in the back of the head. "Everyone starts somewhere."

"I know, but, seriously?" Ro's voice has humor in it.

"What do you mean, 'team with the most Future Fate'? What does that even mean?" Stella glances between the two of them.

"It means," Ro began, "that you four are going to be the most successful Hunters in the world!"

"What?" Rain blurts.

"Well," Mikaya shrugs, "it's technically theoretical, and your Future Fate isn't even supposed to be known, it's a secret, but the word is that the council hand-picked you guys from the same exact school in some place in Pennsylvania. All the other Hunters volunteered and went through this super-hard test in the beginning with the Councilors to see if they would get anywhere if they trained. But the council picked you guys specifically because of what they saw in the future. So, yeah, everyone knows you, and you guys theoretically have the most Future Fate. Maybe we can learn something from you guys."

"Alright, hot shots," Z says from in front of Ro. "I'm not sure if you should go that far. We barely know each other and we're probably terrible at this whole Hunter thing."

"For now," Ro says, and with that, the teacher walks into the room, an old woman with white hair in a bun and glasses connected to a chain around her neck. She wears a dress with a cardigan around it.

"Hello, everybody," the teacher says. "Who would like to learn about imps?"

CHAPTER 13

I walk toward the training wing from the Oriens wing, heading up the stairs to where the training rooms are. I officially hated Imps and that teacher. The class wasn't 'cool' like Z says it is, it's boring. An hour and a half of my life wasted on useless knowledge I'll probably never use. Well, I'll use it on the job, but even then, I could have gotten the point faster. Take out a Goph gun, or a Goph serum, aim at the Imps, put it into their bloodstream, and then you're done. Boom. Easy. So why did we have to train for another hour and a half when I could have been practicing my piano or my singing. It just didn't make any sense to me.

I'm still going to try, though. Even if it is annoying and stupid. For the sake of mankind and for my new acquaintances. I still don't consider them my friends. I have to remember that more than ever because I would catch myself having a somewhat of a good time with them when I didn't even want to. It doesn't matter at the moment, because we're about to go upstairs and train together to try to become the group with the most 'Fate,' whatever that means. The two other kids, Mikaya and Ro, are going upstairs too, but I don't think they're going to train in our group.

I get to the top first and wait for the rest of them to come up behind me. Milo takes the lead and goes to the middle of the room, where a desk sits with a lady behind it, her chin resting on her hand. We walk up to her.

"Hi," Milo greets. "We're here for training. I'm not sure if we check in or something?"

The lady gives Milo a once-over. "Your group doesn't need to check in, we know who you are. Those two, on the other hand, I don't know."

The two look at each other and walk forward. Mikaya speaks. "I'm Mikaya and this is Ro. We're in the same class as them." She points at our group.

"Oh, you're right here," the woman says, pointing at the paper. "Both of you guys are in that room over there." She points to a door to the right. "Good luck."

I stand corrected, I guess they are training with us.

The six of us exchange glances and go to the door. When we walk inside two men are standing with bored looks on their faces. When they see us they perk up a bit.

"Hey, come on in," the first one says. He has black hair slicked to the side. "Don't be scared, we don't bite."

The second one doesn't say anything but starts to set up six similar-looking machines at the far wall. They were slabs of metal that I assume you lay on, connecting to a heart monitor with headsets at the top of the beds.

"I'm Carlos, and this is Tony, the Academy's virtual mentors" the first man, Carlos, says. He seems to do most of the talking. "This is a virtual reality room. We usually use it to make sure you know everything about the creature, demon, or ghost you're studying before you go on assignments, but for the first week, we do it before training. Don't worry, everything you see in this simulation is fake and can't hurt you, but the real training simulations give you pain experiences, which is why we do it before training the first day, to make sure you have absolutely everything down. All you have to do is make it through and defeat the creature you're facing in the simulation with your team. Now, the simulation headsets-"

I stop listening to him and watch the man in the back, Tony. He turns on each heart monitor and headset. He then turns on a computer closer to the group and types something out and watches the screen. He seems satisfied because he carries on by turning off the light by the door.

"Ah, it seems Tony is ready," Carlos says. "Come on, then."

We each set off to a different metal slab. Upon further inspection, I realize there are cuffs to keep the hands and feet in place. With a shiver I lay down on the cold metal as Tony slides the headset on me. He then moves on to put someone else's on. After a bit the two men sound like they have come to the middle again.

"Now just remember to imagine yourself doing the things, like how you would in a dream, and your simulation self will do them." It was Tony this time, his voice deeper than Carlos's.

A click resounds through the room, sounding a lot like a computer. Suddenly, a room appears in my mind. The walls I can barely see from how dark it is, and the ground seems to just be gravel. I gag at the mildew smell. I try to remind myself it's just a simulation at first, but then my brain can't help itself and I start to panic. I can't think of anything except for this room. I go forward a bit when a creature appears from the shadows.

It's a short thing, probably a few feet tall, and it has bat-like wings, a long tail, very long horns, and battish ears. A forked tongue slithered out of its cruel mouth like a snake's. It's green and even more foul smelling than the room.

An Imp.

I survey the room again. On the far left side is a Goph mixture, sitting ominously on a rickety old table. I lunge for it and snatch it up, but just as I look back the Imp disappears into the darkness. I swear under my breath as I hear it swishing around the room. Sliding under the table, I take cover.

The Imp flies straight at my table and shakes it, trying to scare me. Panicking even more, I crawl out from under the table and scramble back up as I run toward the other side of the room. I hear the imp follow me. I start running in a circle around the perimeter of the small space like a cartoon character. I have no clue what to do. It goes on for a few minutes until I finally come up with an idea.

I keep running and suddenly spin around. The Imp tries to stop so it doesn't fly straight into me, but I'm more focused on the Imp's neck. I stick the serum into its throat and press the button that puts the serum in the bloodstream. The Imp fades away into ash and so does the serum holder. Then the room disappears.

I sit up straight and yank my headset off. I'm startled to see everyone watching me. I quickly jump off the machine and awkwardly stand, looking at Tony and Caros. I realize that while I was probably getting chased around the room, everyone was watching me flail around like a crazy person. I gulp.

"Okay, now that everybody made it without injuries or failures..." Carlos looks at me then back at the group. "I guess you all passed. Easy as pie, right? Anyway, that took about a half hour so you still got another hour to train hands on. Then after you're ready your team does your real final simulation with real pain. Then you can finally move on to the next class. Fun times. Okay, off you all go."

We make our way out. Milo leads the group and walks up to the front desk again.

"Hello again, ma'am. We're done with the simulation an-"

"First door to your right is for Oriens," the grumpy woman says.

"Oh," Milo leads the group to the said door. He opens it up and goes inside. One group is training, and I don't recognize them. Maybe they're that Undercover group, Red Riders or something? They're beating up dummies or bench pressing or using Goph. We walk toward the woman and man that seem to be in charge.

"Excuse me, we're new here, do we need to sign in?"

The two look at each other. They were both muscular and looked like they could throw all of us across the room. "I guess you could, what's your group's names?"

"I'm M-"

"We're the TU Crew!" Z interrupts, putting his fists on his hips.

The woman suppresses a grin. "Your actual names, please?"

"As I was saying," Milo glares at Z. "I'm Milo Maeda. These guys are Rain Farley, Zain Montes, and Estelle Booker. Those two are Ro and Mikaya. They aren't part of our team but are our friends. Is it okay if..." Milo trails off and stares around the room. The Red Riders are rushing to get up and out of the room. He frowns.

"Ah, don't mind them," the woman says. "They just are intimidated by you probably. Makes sense."

"Oh," Milo straightens and looks back at her. "Well, is it okay if our friends train with us?"

The woman couldn't hide her smile that time. "Of course they can."

"Alright, thank you." Milo walks off. We disperse across the room. I immediately go to the treadmill and put it on a low setting. I get on and walk, the steps of my feet making me zone out.

Well, zoning out until Z comes onto the treadmill beside her. He turns it onto a run. Then he looks over at me.

"Shouldn't you be going faster?" he asks. "I mean, you were pretty slow back in the simulation."My mouth drops and I glare at him. "What the hell is that supposed to mean? Who are you to tell me what to do?"

Z reaches over and pumps up her treadmill a few levels. "Well, if you want to get better you have to push yourself. It's not enough to just know what to do, you have to do it too." He smiles at himself. "That made no sense. Hold on, let me think of an example. What do you like to do?"

I look at him out of the corner of my eye. The absolute nerve. I just sigh and answer: "Piano."

"Okay, I can work with that." He thinks for a moment. "Let's say you have this really complex piece. What's a complex piece?"

"La Campanella. I've been trying to do it for two years and I'm barely close."

"Wow, okay," he shakes his head. "Anyway, let's say you know all the notes and chords to this La Camp and Ella. You know all of them but haven't even practiced, so you go around and say you know how to play it, and all of your friends think that's really cool, so they want you to come over and play it for them. Then you get there and sit down at a piano and fail miserably because you've never actually played the piece. Then all your friends dump you because they're fake and annoying and are using you." I give him a look. "Anyway, my point is, if you know how to do everything but haven't actually done it, it doesn't count. The only way you know how to do something is if you've done it before. So do it."

I stare at him. That one also didn't really make much sense, but it was better than the one before. This is a dangerous game I'm playing. These people were really counting on me. I didn't want to be dropped by them, which made no sense, I wasn't even friends with them. Instead of answering I look down at my feet and watch as they pound, pound, pound against the treadmill.

By the time I look up again, Z's gone.

CHAPTER 14

The rest of the week is basically the same as that first day but without the long Simulation. Well, we did have the final simulation together yesterday, and both groups passed, barely, with a few scratches and pains. I do think Stella's acting kind of odd, though. I expected her to warm up a little bit more. Everybody else's friendships kicked off instantly. Stella acts like she did when they all first met, if not then colder. She almost made us lose the final simulation, maybe on purpose? The thing with Stella, I think, is that she's too hung up over her other friends. She still sits with them and talks to them and spends most of her free time with them. It doesn't make sense to me.

I learned over the week a few things that I should take note of. The first is that speakers of different languages were on the two other planets. Ecsporavet was the smallest 'planet' and was only for those who could speak English fluently. The other planets had different languages and different Academies that were copies of the English Academy, except in different languages.

The pink planet was called Ezhitaria. It has Spanish, German, French, Russian, Arabic, Thai, and Lakota. The multi-colored planet was called Sealgare. It has African, Chinese, Mandarin,

Japanese, Hebrew, and Greek. The red planet was called Venandias. It has Irish, Italian, Latin, Portuguese, Vietnamese, Persian, and Malay. If someone didn't know one of those languages, they couldn't become a Hunter. I, personally, think this is unfair, but I can't really change it.

The reason English is alone is because it's the most widely spoken language so it has to be the biggest, and the English Academy probably looked a bit weird next to these small Academies, so they just separated it altogether, apparently. Also doesn't really make sense to me, but, once again, I can't really change it.

Ecsporavet is also really cold, like we literally shouldn't be able to even move because of how far from this solar system's sun we are, but it's just another thing our do for us. Gravity is also weird on Ecsporavet, too. We should be flying off into space with how little gravity is on this floating, fake rock, but we don't because of our necklaces. It makes the planet have about the same amount of gravity as the moon. It also orbits the biggest planet, Venandias, like a moon.

Tomorrow will be our first weekend day, which means we would have more time and would get lunch at the Academy. Today was also our first day with Shedims. We also might be getting our first assignment. Today is, also, Friday the 13th. I hope this doesn't mean anything foreboding as I walk to our usual alleyway and find everyone waiting outside the opening.

"Sunshine!" Z exclaims. He holds out a fist and I bump it with mine. Z's voice gets deeper and takes on an announcer tone. "Are you ready to rumble?" He holds out the last word like he's on WWE, that old program where a bunch of people fought each other in an obviously staged manner. Things before the Outbreak were almost weirder than they are now.

"Depends. Are you ready to actually be quiet and listen during the lectures?" I cross my arms.

"Also depends on if the lecture is boring or not," Z replies. "Professor-Snooze-Lady couldn't hold an audience of stuffed animals. Come on, let's go meet our new teacher."

Z leads the way into the small room. I make a mental note to clean it out and maybe add in some more furniture in the future. I look behind me to make sure Stella and Milo are coming through the corridor. When I look back, the portal is open and Z's gone. I enter the portal and get sucked into Ecsporavet.

I'm used to the journey by now, so when I'm sucked back into existence I don't lose my balance. Z's walking up the path at a steady pace and I hurry to follow. Soon, we're all in the Oriens wing. Alexander is also there, holding out papers to us.

"Good job on the first week, guys," Alexander says, handing us the small stack. "There's the schedule for this week. I'm very impressed with you guys. You can go on ahead to this week's class."

Milo beams and sets off to the room. The rest of us hurry to follow. Alexander clears his throat and our gazes turn back to him.

"Not you, Stella," he says. "I need to talk to you about... something."

Stella hesitantly follows him as he walks away. Me and Z exchange glances and follow Milo to the room. Ro and Mikaya are already there, talking about some sort of infestation. We fill in these chairs as we did the week before.

"Whatcha talking about?" I ask, leaning in.

"There's this small Imp infestation at a house in Chicago," Ro fiddles with a pen. "We were pretty sure it's gonna be you guys who take care of it."

"That doesn't make sense, though," Z says, leaning back in his chair. "Stella was terrible, I think Alexander's talking some sense into her. He'll probably do a better job than us, at least."

"Exactly," Milo says. "If anything it's gonna be you guys."

Mikaya looks him up and down. "Whatever you say, man." She winks and turns back to Ro. I shift in my seat, looking back at Milo. I feel irrationally jealous. I study him. Milo gives me an odd look that's difficult to read.

"What?" I ask.

"Nothing," he says, clearing his throat. "Just wondering."

I watch him a bit longer then turn forward just as Stella walks through the door. She takes her seat beside Z. He looks at her for a moment then leans in.

"What was that about?" he whispers. I strain to listen.

"Nothing," she says curtly.

"What happened?" he asks.

"Nothing," she replies again in the same tone. She set her bag onto the desk with a smack. That seems to declare the end of the conversation because Z shuts up quickly. I slump lower into my chair. There was no way we were getting the Imp assignment if we couldn't communicate.

The professor comes in, a middle aged man with a beard and mustache. He sets his stuff down and surveys us.

"Hello," he greets, "I'm professor Mac-"

There was a hurried knock at the door. The professor opens it and in comes Alexander. He looks straight at us. "You four have an assignment. Hurry up."

"Told you," Ro sing-songs.

Milo begrudgingly stands up. We stand, too. We walk out the door and follow Alexander to the training wing. I look back one last time at the professor's confused face and the other two's smug ones.

Alexander heads up the stairs in the training wing and the group comes up behind him. Right behind the staircase leading up is a door that's marked "Assignments." Alexander uses his IDHS bracelet to open the door. It beeps and he pushes it open. What greets us is a big white room.

Lining the walls are weapons of all kinds, Goph serums, Goph Guns, normal guns, knives, Goph Knives, Phors, bows and arrows, Goph arrows, spears, Goph spears, and basically every other weapon you could think of with a Goph counterpart. In the back is a hallway with rooms along the walls. We wander to the middle of the room, where a big machine is sitting, a tube stretching towards the ceiling.

He strides toward the machine and taps a few buttons. A whirring noise and then a few shapes zip down the tube quickly, so quickly I can't see what they are. He opens a compartment and takes out some IDHS Uniforms and boots.

He holds them out to us. "Change in those rooms back there." He points to the hallway in the back.

Z grabs the uniforms and holds each one out to us. They each have our names on the collars. We rush back and each pick our own room. I enter mine, one more towards the back of the hall, and study the uniform.

Of course I already know what it looks like from the media, but there are so many more details up close. There is a black cargo jumpsuit, along with a cropped, fitted black shirt with no sleeves and black tights. The black combat boots are grippy and sturdy as well. For the arms there are sleeves that aren't connected to the shirt and green cuffs at the end. I pull the shirt, tights, and sleeves on and then go for the jumpsuit.

It's made out of a breathable but thick material that seems unlike anything I had felt before. On the collar is my name and the IDHS symbol. Upon closer inspection I realize that the inside of the fabric is green and the ends of the belt, the flap on the chest pockets, and a strip on the middle buttons is green as well. I slip it on and do the belt on the waist, then do the buttons leading up to my throat. I put on the combat boots and double knot the laces. Then I straighten up, look at myself in the mirror, take a deep breath, and step outside the room.

Milo and Z are already out of the changing room in their uniforms, looking at something Alexander is holding to them. "These are helmets you will be using to disguise yourselves out in the world. We do want you to be undercover, after all." Alexander hands the helmets out to them and then to me. It looks like a biker helmet, black with a green IDHS symbol on the side. The signature undercover helmet. I put it on and realize that the visibility is amazing, which is surprising, since from the outside it looks completely black.

"The helmets allow you to communicate with each other, all you have to do is tap the right side of your helmet and it should put your vision onto all of your teammates' visors, as well as transmit your voice to them. You can turn it off by clicking the button again."

I test the button, as do Milo and Z, and two squares show up on the right of my visor, me at two different angles. I hate to say it, but I do look really cool.

"Awesome!" Z exclaims, looking around the room at a dizzying speed.

Just then Stella walks out of her changing room, the top of the jumpsuit unbuttoned and hanging at her hips. It makes it look stylish. She looks as smug as a cat as she takes a helmet and puts it on. Alexander looks at her outfit choice and his lips thin into a straight line. "You do know that the fabric is reinforced so it's almost impossible to rip, you should really button it back up."

"I like it better this way, more breathable," Stella retorts, crossing her arms. She taps the button on her helmet and her screen pops up under Milo's and Z's.

Alexander looks at her for a beat. "Fine. Suit yourself. We really should be going, though. We're already late."

With that, he walks back to the main room and gets us each a Goph Gun. They look like handguns, but I know better. There are bullets of Goph in here that could enter a demon's bloodstream and kill them. There are other weapons, I know that from training, but Goph Guns are all we can be trusted with right now.

Alexander then heads to the end of the hallway and opens a door there. Outside is a big gateway to earth. He turns back to us. "This is the Launch Pad, where all groups go through to get to earth on assignments. Pay attention. This is the first assignment, so it shouldn't be anything too difficult. When you get to Chicago, you will go to this address," he hands a piece of paper to Milo, "and take care of the infestation. They're just Imps and shouldn't be too hard to take care of, but be careful either way. And, above all else, communicate." He throws a pointed look in Stella's direction. "Also, whatever you do, do not panic. Demons can sense fear and they prey off of it." He steps aside and motions to the gateway. "Goodluck."

Milo reads the address on the paper and looks up, a look of concentration on his face.

"When I go through, will the portal stay the same for them?" he says with a motion toward us.

A nod from Alexander is all he needs. He steps through the swirling portal without looking back.

CHAPTER 15

I'm going to end up dead by the rate Milo is going. The moment everyone got their bearings he started running towards the street.

The portal dropped us off on the sidewalk of a busy street, startling a poor lady so much she almost fell. We didn't have time to apologize to her before Milo ran off. We hastily followed him through the busy streets of Chicago, Illinois. Chicago's in a different time zone than us, so we're now an hour behind our usual time, also meaning it's currently almost three. Now, we finally get to the address, a three-story apartment complex in the suburbs, and we're all out of breath and panting, except, of course, for Milo.

"Come on, you guys, we don't have all day," Milo chides.

"Don't we get a van or something?" Stella asks between breaths.

"We get a van when we complete at least three assignments." Milo walks up to the front door. He pushes it open and peers inside. It's completely dark. Stella zips up her cargo suit with a gulp.

"Ready?" Milo asks.

"Born ready or whatever," I respond, walking up behind him.

We go inside and all collectively start coughing. The room is dusty and so dark it takes my eyes a few minutes to adjust. There's, thankfully, nobody around. The ceiling to the first floor has fallen and debris is everywhere. The lights are busted except for one on the second floor. The elevators and stairs are blocked so we have to go up on a piece of the second floor, making a very unstable ramp.

"Classy," I grumble, almost tripping on a stray piece of rock.

"Shut up," Stella whispers curtly.

"Oh, what, the imps will hear us? I think we already gave that away from the sound of your worrying."

"I'm not worrying."

"Right, of course you aren't."

"Would both of you be quiet?" Rain mumbles. "I can't hear the sound of my own thoughts."

"Now you decide to talk?" Stella demands. She has a point, Rain has been awfully quiet.

"I just want to make sure-"

"Stop," Milo whispers. "I hear something."

"Of course you do!" I yell. "What's up with you and your-"

"No. Actually. Be quiet." Milo stands rigidly, staring up to the second floor. We shut up quickly. He slowly climbs a few steps and peeks up over the floor. After a second he looks back at us.

"I think we're goo-"

A shape flies down at us at top speed, smacking Rain in the side. She loses her balance but is quickly righted by Stella. I grab my gun from my belt and point it at the shape. It gets up quickly, and I'm startled to see an Imp there, a small gremlin- looking thing with small wings and tiny horns. It looks up at me and a mischievous smile spreads across its face. I yelp and pull the trigger on my gun. Unfortunately, I'm not necessarily the best shot.

The bullet ricochets off the drywall ramp and flies off into the darkness of the first floor. The Imp lunges straight for me. A shot echoes in the darkness and the Imp seems to stop flying, but it still has enough momentum that it crashes into my chest. I fall backward and land on my back, head pointing towards the first floor.

The Imp on my chest cries out and dissolves into ash-looking dust. I scramble up and wipe off my shirt quickly, but not before another Imp comes flying down, straight towards Milo this time. He aims at the Imp and shoots, the bullet flying right in between the eyes. The Imp dissolves in another puff of dust.

We sit in silence for a second. That moment felt significant to me, the first demons we've ever killed. Well, more like that Milo killed. Those were people once, so we basically just killed someone for the second time.

"Alright, that must be all of them they sent." Milo looks up to the second floor. "Let's keep moving."

We make the trek to the second floor and assess the area. The stairs are thankfully unblocked, but some of the apartments aren't. We decide to check the ones that are open. The search comes back negative, so we enter the stairwell.

"Maybe there were only two?" Rain hopes.

"Maybe." Milo climbs the staircase quickly, only stopping at the top to wait for us. "I'm going in first to scan the area. If I don't come back in thirty seconds, assume I'm fighting a bunch of Imps."

We agree and he opens the door, only for a dozen small Imps to ambush him. He stumbles back into the stairwell, almost falling down the stairs. I raise my gun and shoot a couple of times, getting one down. Rain and Stella are shooting too, getting about three. Milo is blindly shooting around at the cloud around him, somehow not hitting any of us. Just when the numbers start to come down, a new hoard comes from the third floor. I'm running out of ammo, and from the increasingly worried looks on Stella and Rain's faces, it looks like they are too. It seems pointless.

"Fall back?" I shout, the Imps surrounding all of us now.

"Fall back!" Milo agrees, and I race down the stairs three at a time, followed by everyone else. I bolt down the second floor corridor and slide down the ramp. I trip in the lobby and sprawl onto the floor. Rain kneels down and grabs my hand, pulling me up while simultaneously running. Stella pulls the door open and holds it, ushering us out. Milo stops and turns, picking off a few Imps dangerously close to us. Rain bolts out the door and I'm close behind her. Milo leaves next, with Stella slamming the door shut behind him.

We step back from the door, warily watching it. There are a few BANGS from inside, but the door holds. I sit down on the sidewalk in exasperation and look around. At this point multiple people are watching us, all with equally terrified, confused, and awe-struck looks on their faces. I sigh and hang my head.

"Thanks for the help, Sunshine," I say before I can think about it.

"No problem," Rain mumbles back, still staring at the door.

"Well, I guess that's that," Stella murmurs, turning from the house. I dejectedly get up and start to follow her.

"We gave it all we could," Rain says to Milo, putting her hand on his shoulder. Then she turns around and follows us.

"No."

We all stop and look back at him. He spins around and stares at us. "You guys are just giving up? We weren't put on this mission to give up. We came on this mission to get rid of those Imps. We are not going back until we get rid of these things. Let's go."

"What?" Stella looks like she wants to kill him. "We nearly died in there. I am not going against something I can't beat. I'm accepting that some- times things don't go my way. I would have expected you to accept that too!"

"But we can beat these things. We're prepared this time, we know what we're up against. I am the leader of this group and I am not accepting defeat. Now let's. Go."

I look between them. They both have good points, we did almost die in there. Whether we like it or not we aren't ready for this, but Milo is our leader. We can't leave without him, and something's telling me he isn't going to leave.

Reluctantly, I go to his side. Rain follows my lead and we all look at Stella. She glares at us and sighs.

"I knew this whole Hunter thing was going to get me killed," she grumbles.

CHAPTER 16

These people are absolutely insane. I should never have become a Hunter-In-Training. That's what I keep telling myself as we go back to the door. No way are they actually going back into the place that almost killed them. Sometimes I think I'm the only sane person in the world.

Milo walks up to the door and pulls out his gun. He opens the door and immediately whips his gun up. The sound must have alert the Imps, because dead silence emits from the building. Milo hesitantly walks in, the rest of us right behind him. Nothing moves in the dark, nothing comes straight for us. The Imps were right here, weren't they?

Milo goes up the ramp at a slow pace, squinting in the dark. I take a deep breath and follow the group up. There doesn't seem to be any demons on the second floor, they must have all gravitated toward the safest place, the third floor.

We go into the stairwell. I can feel the nervous energy through the group. I pull my gun out of my belt as we climb the stairs.

We wait by the door and, with a deep breath, Milo pushes it open. Nothing comes through.

"What?" Z questions. "Where did they all go?"

"Maybe they all got scared?" Rain ventures. No one responds this time. She slowly goes through the threshold. Not one form smashes into her.

"Is there roof access?" Milo asks.

"I don't think so." Rain disappears into the dark. A moment later she comes back. "None."

"Great," I grumble, getting mad. "So we didn't even have to come back in here. Thanks a lot, everyone. Made me scared for nothing."

"How is this our fault? You're the one who decided to come with us." Z steps closer to me.

"It's not like I had a choice. What was I supposed to do, sit around on the sidewalk with the news reporters while you did all the work?"

"Can you guys stop?" Milo crosses his arms. "The Imps are most definitely still in this building, unless they disappeared, which I highly doubt. We are going to find them and finish this assignment."

"Let's get going, then," I say, storming to the stairwell.

CHAPTER 17

The first time I saw the group of teenagers who changed my life was when they were in the middle of a heated argument. Not the best first impression, believe me. They were on the second floor of Sunset Apartments, standing by the stairwell, yelling about why they were here and arguing about not communicating. It was really surprising, I thought I was getting a group that would save my sorry self, and that's saying a lot. I was a very sorry self.

I was alone that night, just myself and the Imps. I sent them back, though. They did their job well. My mission was pretty simple: try to get them on our side.

I stepped out of the shadows. The first person to notice me was the short, feminine figure. It was mildly infuriating that I couldn't see their faces underneath their helmets. She stared at me. I stared at her. The boy that was the tallest noticed me next. The other two, a shorter boy and a taller girl, were still in the middle of the argument, screaming at each other.

"Guys," the boy who had noticed me said, "look."

The other boy begrudgingly looked up and I assumed he went pale. A similar reaction with the girl. I smiled at them.

"Who are you?" the first boy asked. He appeared to be the leader of the group.

"My name is Lucifer," I said, lifting my arms. "One of the seven princes of the Underworld."

When I say this to people they usually run in fear or laugh at my face. This group, though, they did nothing. Just stared at me some more.

"So, where did the Imps go?" The other boy asked. "You see we're kind of trying to do an assignment for the Academy? Do you know what that is?"

I looked at him. "Yes, Hunter, I know what the Academy is. It is only the bane of my existence. That is not the main point right now, though. What I am trying to tell you is that I am Lucifer, yes that Lucifer, and I am here to recruit you to our side."

"No," the taller girl informed. She took out her gun and pointed it at me. "We're not going anywhere with you."

This seemed to snap them out of their staring trance, because they too took out their guns and aimed them at me.

I laughed. "Cute."

My shadows expanded toward them, hungry, ravenous. This is just a bluff, but I need to make it convincing. I would never actually kill them, I just needed them to think I would.

"I can stop this if you come with me," I informed them, walking closer. "You have no need to be afraid if you just surrender." To prove my point, I let my shadows lick against the feet of the leader boy.

A couple of beats of silence passed. The shorter boy raised his hand. "Can we get a group huddle?"

"No."

"Oh."

A couple more seconds of quiet.

"Alright, fine," the leader exasperated. "I'll bite. What do you want from us?"

"Your help, actually." I shifted. "We are in desperate need of your help."

"Why on earth would you tell us that?" The leader looked at me suspiciously. "Also, who's we?"

I silently curse myself. Negotiating isn't really my strong suit.

"I need you to trust me," I venture.

"Why would we do that when you're using your witchy powers on us?" the taller girl asked. "Fat chance. Just leave us alone. We aren't going anywhere with you."

"Wait," the leader stepped forward. "We'll go. Just don't hurt us please." He glanced at the taller girl.

Something was wrong.

They shouldn't just trust me this easily.

I stared at him. I could play this game. "Come with me." I turned toward the shadows. Too late, I remember that I shouldn't turn my back on people that don't trust me. A force slammed into me from behind. It's not enough to actually do anything, but I decided to play along. I stumbled, and the force kicked the back of my legs. I purposefully fell rather ungracefully, sprawled on the ground. It's only a second, for I jumped up right away, but it's enough time for them to be sprinting towards the ramp.

I don't know what made me stop and watch them, maybe the fact that I could get them at any time I wanted, or maybe I wanted the word to spread. Maybe I just wanted them to have a slight chance at oblivious- ness until they couldn't anymore. But I watched them bolt out the lobby and crash through the doors.

I sighed and sank back into the shadows.

CHAPTER 18

As soon as we leave the apartment complex we run. I have no clue if that Lucifer guy is still following us or not, but we sprint through the streets until we finally get to a secluded alley.

"What. Was. That." Rain gets this out between breaths, hunched over with her hands on her knees.

"I'm not sure, but we probably need to get this back to Alexander quick." Stella holds up her hand and summons a portal.

"Wait," I say. "We failed the assignment. We were supposed to take out the Imps. We didn't. We have to go bac-"

"Would you shut up about this assignment?!" Stella shouts. It makes me flinch from how loud and cruel her words are. Stella's not usually mean. It makes me stop and listen. "We almost died. Twice. That guy said he said he was Lucifer! Y'know, a literal prince of the Underworld?! We are definitely not qualified for that. What don't you get? We don't have to do everything perfectly. I backed down to you once, I am not doing it again." She steps back into her portal and disappears with a whoosh.

"Sorry, man, I'm with her on this. There's no way we're going to survive if we go there a second time." He looks to Rain and steps through the portal.

I turn to my last hope, Rain, and stare at her.

"You can't seriously expect me to agree with you on this, right?" She shakes her helmeted head. "Let's go tell Alexander."

I turn around, accepting the fact I'll be alone on this. "I'm not leaving this assignment unfinished. I accept if you don't want to join me, that's your cho-"

She pushes me into the portal with surprising strength. I travel through time and space, and get pushed out on the other side. I'm so shocked I don't have time to catch myself before I fall to the ground on Ecsporavet. Stella and Z are there, staring at me. I just have time to scramble out of the way before Rain comes through. She lands gracefully on her feet. I stare at her in surprise.

"There was no way I was leaving you there alone." She holds out a hand and I begrudgingly take it as Stella closes the portal. No point going back now. I look around for the first time and realize we're at the Launch Pad. I take off into the Academy, immediately seeking Alexander out. I find him in the training wing, leaning against a wall. He notices me and walks forward.

"Milo!" he waves at me. "Glad to see you back. Did everything go smoothly?"

"Well, that's exactly what-"

"No, don't tell me. I'm not allowed to know. Not sure why I asked. Go straight to the Councilors."

"The Councilors? Why?"

"They want to know how every assignment goes. If I were you, I would disclose any and all information. They need to know how the assignments go."

"Don't they already know?"

"I suppose they do, but they can't really be bothered to go looking for each detail specifically. It's a long process to use See."

"See?" I question.

"The process for seeing the past or the future. They can't disclose how they do it, but they aren't usually wrong about much. Sometimes seeing the future is iffy, though, so they don't usually do it in case they change the future in some drastic way. That is, if they don't tell-"

"Okay, we get it," Z says, surprising me. I didn't know they were there. "Can we just go to the councilors now?"

"Yes," Alexander says, walking to the stairs. "Just make sure you don't... say too much."

"What do you mean?" Rain asks. "How would we say too much if-"

"Just be careful," Alexander interrupts.

On that cheerful note, we trudge up the stairs to the very top of the training wing. The councilors' door is the only thing on this level, besides the door to the balcony. It's looming ominously at the top of the stairs. Its metal shine blinds me as we get closer. Alexander uses his bracelet to scan the door. It slides open with a hiss, revealing the semicircle of chairs that the councilors are sitting in. The chairs are raised and behind a desk, four of them in total, each holding a person watching us with blank expressions. They must have not been expecting us, because they seem to be interrupted. We enter the room and stand before them.

"Welcome, Alexander," the woman with the slick-backed, blonde ponytail says. She looks to be around forty, with piercing blue eyes and pale skin. She sports black robes, the same as all the other councilors, making her look somewhat like a judge. Her name tag on her desk reads 'Atara.' "What business?"

"This group of Hunters has just gotten back from a mission," Alexander reports.

Hunters. Not Hunters-in-Training, but fully certified Hunters. We have experience. A small grin comes onto my face before I can smother it.

"What's the group's name?" a man with long, black hair asks. Griffin, based on his name tag, looks fairly younger than Atara, maybe twenties? He has a darker complexion and an intimidating face.

I fully grin this time. "The TU Crew."

I feel Z fist-pump in the air behind me.

A woman that looks around the same age as the long-haired man flips through a few papers. She has brown hair and an almond skin tone. She looks like she would be kind, but she has a frown on her face like she would rather be anywhere else but there. Her name tag has swirls doodled onto it and it reads 'Lottie' in a cursive font. She flips through them for a couple of seconds before she looks up. "There is no group with that name here. Names? We'll make a record for you."

We give them our names and they make a record. They seem a bit shocked at our names, like they know something we don't. I assume it's from the 'Fate', or whatever Mikaya and Ro said.

"Well, let's hear it," an older man says. His name is Graham, and he looks like he's sixty, with graying hair and glasses. He has pale skin that's wrinkling. "What happened on your assignment?"

We explain what happened. They become increasingly pale as I describe Lucifer, my friends chiming in when necessary.

"Let me get this straight," Lottie says when we're done. "Lucifer, like one of the seven princes of the Underworld Lucifer, came to you guys on an Imp assignment, told you he needed his help and that he was going to take you to the Underworld, and you somehow managed to get away from him unscathed?"

"That sums it up, yeah," Z adds.

"I don't believe it for a second." She looks around at the councilors. "There is no possible way. This is the first time this has happened to any of our Hunters, I say they're lying. Plus, they couldn't have gotten away. He's more powerful than all of them combined, quadrupled."

"Stop, Lottie," Griffin interrupts. "There's a first time for everything. Besides, this group has the most Future Fate out of any of our Hunter groups, if it can happen to anyone, it can happen to them."

There it is again, the Future Fate. It's scary to think that if we don't live up to that expectation, we very well could be useless.

Lottie stares at him and sighs. "I still want to use See on this, Griffin. If these kids are lying, we're going to find out."

"The fact of the matter isn't if they are right or not," Atara chimes in, "it's if we should be concerned. If they aren't lying, and that's a big if, then we need to make sure they are safe; that their lives aren't in danger by being Hunters any more than the next group. We'll have to tell you guys next time you come. In the meantime, please go home and rest. I have a feeling you all might need it."

CHAPTER 19

I step out of the councilors' room with my friends and head to the stairs. I want nothing more than to go home, but Elsie has other plans. She told me to meet her at the school at the soonest chance. I informed her that I couldn't get there soon and, at the very earliest, I could get there at five. It was currently six thirty, and I could already hear her voice telling me that she had been waiting 'forever'. I couldn't imagine what she wanted me at the school for, or why she wanted to talk to me so formally anyway. Couldn't she just text me?

We get to the portal entrance outside. Ecsporavet was set up with Megicusus in a way that no one could make portals unless they were in select designated areas, like the main entrance or the Launch Pad. Milo holds up his hand and makes a portal. We step through and end up at our designated portal alley. There is, expectedly, no one around. I immediately take off down the street to the school.

"Hey!" Z runs up beside me. "Where are you going in such a hurry?"

"None of your business," I grumble. The nerve of some people. One second he's yelling at me in Chicago, the next he's wanting to know where I'm going in Pennsylvania.

"As your teammate and your friend, I think it is my business. You look like you're heading to the school?"

"First of all, I'm not your friend-"

"Sureeee."

"And second, I'm meeting somebody there. So if you wouldn't mind going home."

"Oh, I'm not going home. Not for a while, anyway. Might as well come with you."

"Wait," I look at him, "what do you mean, you're not going home?"

"Who are you meeting, anyway?" he asks, his smile faltering. "Is it your boyfriend?"

He drags the last word out. I can sense the quick subject change. I can tell he doesn't want to talk about it, so I welcome it. "No. I'm meeting my friend. Don't ask me why at the school and don't ask me why we're meeting in the first place. I have no clue."

"Huh, guess you beat me to the punch." He kicks a pebble on the road and a few beats of silence pass. We get a few blocks down the road when he says: "Why are you so mad at me, anyway? What did I do to you?"

I look at him. "You're just..." I pause.

Why am I so mad at him?

Is it because he insulted my friends? Maybe. Is it because he insulted me? Also maybe. Is it because he was annoying? Yet again, maybe.

The real reason, though?

I'm scared.

So scared. Terrified that maybe he doesn't actually care about me. Terrified that I might see him as a friend when he saw me as a means to an end. Maybe if I opened up to him, he would shove it back in my face, and it would be the last time I opened up ever again.

But, above all, I was scared he would leave me.

In freshman year, ninth grade, I met this guy named Rowan. He was a senior, with really dark black hair, brown eyes, tall, and super handsome. He had this mysterious bad boy esc to him that made all the girls swoon over him. He specifically talked to the freshman, which, looking back, was kind of creepy, but I loved it at the time. Thought I was special. I thought I loved him. He said he loved me. It was the classic story: a girl thinks she's special, a guy thinks he's hot stuff, he takes her virginity, and then spreads the story to the whole school. It took me so long to get those allegations out of the way. The rest of freshman year was the worst, sophomore year wasn't as bad, but I was still brought up in conversation a lot. Junior year was finally the year that I could be normal, I was finally free, and I wasn't going to give that up for the first guy who came along.

I look back at Z. "You're just annoying."

He seems taken aback by this, but he smiles and punches me in the shoulder playfully. "What did you expect?"

"I..." I look down at the sidewalk. "I'm not sure. Maybe someone who doesn't switch up on me."

"Well, I apologize for being annoying," he says in a regal accent, "I will strive for utmost perfection in the near future."

"Shut up," I say with a smile.

He stares at me with a shocked look, like I just told him the world was flat. "Do that again."

"What?" I ask, my smile dropping.

"Laugh," he says, a smile spreading across his face. He sounds like he just saw the sun for the first time in years, like he saw the world light up and he doesn't want it to stop shining ever again.

I look forward quickly and silently thank whoever is in the sky that we are at the school's entrance. There doesn't seem to be anyone around, so I walk right up to the front door. It isn't unlocked, but Elsie taught me a while ago how to pick locks so we wouldn't get in trouble in the halls.

The door is, surprisingly, a simple lock, nothing else needed except for a bobby pin. I drop to my knees in front of it and grab a pin out of my hair. I pick the lock and open the door, Z staring at me the whole time.

"You can go now," I say to him, not wanting him to get in the way of what Elsie wants to tell me.

"After we got this far? No chance, Starlight." He steps through the door I'm holding open.

"Starlight?" I wonder aloud.

"Trying it out," he informs me. "You're just like a star. People don't expect much from you but then you surprise them with the brightest laugh or the coolest hobbies. Plus, Estelle and Stella mean star, right?"

I smile, touched, and walk in after him. "Right."

My parents named me Estelle because it meant star. My mom told me that my dad picked the name out because of my older brother. His name is Aster, which means star as well.

My dad's reasoning was that God sent them two stars to brighten their lives, so they named us as such. My brother is off in college now, but my name is a reminder to me, a reminder of my family. A reminder of my dad.

I was only five when he died, I don't remember him as much as I wish I could, but what I do remember is him being the kindest man alive. Aren't they weird, memories? How sometimes the only thing you have left of someone is how you saw them. How maybe your view of them was clouded by your judgment. Your memories might not even be your memories, they could be stories.

My favorite memory of my dad is when I was four. We were in the grocery store together, and we were just walking out, and on the sidewalk was a woman. She was lying there, sleeping, and I know now that she was homeless.

My dad took one look at her and grabbed a few cans of food from one of our grocery bags. I didn't know what was happening at the time, but he set them gently down beside her. He didn't wake her up or anything, just grabbed my arm and kept on walking to the car.

When I asked him about it in the car, he said something I'd never forget.

"My little Star, there are some people in this world who are less fortunate than us, and I think that we should give up some of our fortune for them, no matter what."

"What if we are the ones who are less fortunate?" I asked him.

"Then we have to rely on other people to show us the same kindness we showed them. It always pays off to be kind, Estelle. Always."

I'm not sure why this moment resonated with me, but who knows why any moment resonates with anybody. This might be the reason I'm not the textbook definition of a popular girl. Maybe I'm nice to everybody because my dad was nice to everybody first.

Z and I walk through the double doors leading to the locker bay. I haven't seen Elsie anywhere in the school, and the fact that I haven't seen any patrol or janitors either makes me nervous. Maybe they're all watching us through the cameras, waiting to see what we get up to. I'm so scared that when Elsie calls my name in a whisper I almost jump out of my skin.

I look around frantically but can't see her. "Elsie? Where are you?"

She steps out from behind a row of lockers and looks at me, a flicker of surprise flashing on her face as she sees Z. Her blonde hair is spilling down her shoulders, her bangs almost covering her blue eyes staring at us as we get closer. She's wearing a black hoodie and jeans. She leans against a locker and frowns at us.

"So, you did bring him," a flash of something crosses her face-disappointment, maybe? Or anger? It's masked quickly behind a smirk. "Maybe you already know why you're here."

"What are you talking about, Elsie? Why did you call me here? No, better question, why here? If you're going to be sneaking around, then a school is not the place to do it. There are cameras everywhere. If you wanted to talk about something, you could have just texted me?"

She shrugs. "At first, I wanted to know where you were going after school, because it wasn't back to your house. Trust me, I tried to ask your mom where you were. She said she thought you were with your friends, which doesn't make sense, since we're the only friends you have. So, I used a tracker in that sweater I gave you. You wore it yesterday, and you went to this weird alley and then your tracker disappeared. It didn't stop, it didn't get deactivated, it disappeared.

"Something was going on, so I started paying attention to you today. You seemed on edge, like you were waiting for something. Or, someone. So, I did what any sensible person would do, and I came here. I have someone I know who works as a patrolman for night, so I just asked him to send me the footage after school. All of it. So, I have blackmail, proof, and you are not leaving this school until you explain, and until you make clean on our bet." She smirks her cat-like smirk and motions for us to get on with it.

My heart drops. The bet. I had forgotten all about it. I was supposed to make someone fall in love with me, and then dump them. I realize with a start that she thinks me and Z are together. That I'm supposed to break his heart. I never stopped to think that I could hurt Z. I stare at Elsie in shock.

"Yes, Stella," she purrs, "I set you up. I expect you to make full on your bet, and explain, or I release the footage to the school and get you and him expelled."

CHAPTER 20

The way this Elsie girl looked right now made me enraged. Like she just won a game Stella didn't know they were playing. Like she was better than her. Like she outsmarted her.

"Why?" Stella croaks, tears coming to her eyes.

"Oh, Stella," Elsie gets closer, "poor, sweet Stella. Don't you get it? I. Never. Liked. You. You're like a dog, no matter how many times you get hurt, you trust the first person to show you the slightest ounce of love. We were never friends. You were nothing but a way to get me higher, a step stool, if you will."

A step stool? A dog? I'm mad now. I don't know what the whole bet is, but there is no way she's getting away with this, and there's no way we're telling her what we've been doing. I step forward and glare at her.

"Don't you ever speak to her like that again. She's so much more than a step stool, or a dog. She's my friend, alright? No one talks to my friends like that. No one. You can take this to the school, for all I care, but you would have to out yourself in the process. Is that something you can handle?"

She laughs in my face. "Haven't you heard of editing, Z?" She says my nickname like the punchline of a joke. "All I'd have to do is remove this whole part and edit it so it only shows you both wandering around. All I want to know is where you went, or how the tracker was disabled, and for Stella to finish a bet."

I look at Stella and search her eyes. "What bet is she talking about, Stella?"

"Oh yes," Elsie giggles, "do tell him."

Stella looks like she's about to throw up. She turns to Elsie. "He's just a friend, Elsie. If I said it to him it would have no effect. There...I...He isn't the type to care, anyway."Elsie shakes her head. "That's not going to work, Stella. Anybody could see the way he looks at you. It doesn't take a detective to know what's going on. Cut the act."

"I mean it," Stella insists. "He barely knows me."

I finally realize that they're talking about me. That I'm the one that looks at her a different way than everyone else.

"Someone who 'barely knows you' wouldn't stand up for you like he did. Face it, Estelle, he likes you."

I stare at Elsie in shock and anger. Not only is she talking to Stella like she's inferior in every way possible, but she's assuming things about me that aren't true.

But, maybe they are.

Maybe I do like Estelle Booker.

No, I realize, I definitely do like Stella.

I like her personality, I like the fact she's defending me, I like the way her curly hair looks in the light, I like her style, I like her name, I like her eyes that shine almost golden in the sun, and I like her.

I like everything about her.

Stella turns to me and she looks like the weight of the world is on her shoulders. She looks like she's scared, and that gives me the courage to look Elsie in the eyes. It gives me the courage to run at her full sprint and lunge at her.

I wouldn't say I attack girls all that often, in fact, I've never hit anybody ever, much less a girl. But something about this last week, training, maybe, has given me the strength to push my hands to Elsie's torso and throw my whole weight behind them.

Elsie stumbles back a bit and falls to the floor, her head hitting the ground in a way that makes me wince. Stella realizes what I'm doing and calls my name, only it sounds like a warning instead of a plea. I look back at her and realize my mistake at the same time Elsie does, because she throws me off of herself with surprising force and hops to her feet. I roll into the lockers on the other side and get to my feet a lot less gracefully than her. Stella realizes the show- down that is about to happen and takes a few steps back.

We stare at each other for a second, her hair now messy. She pulls it back into a ponytail quickly and laughs. "Come at me then, Loverboy. Let's see what you got."

This enrages me more, which is probably what she wants, but I can't find it in myself to care. I charge at her, and she sidesteps me easily. I smack into the lockers and probably get a minor concussion. Her smile grows wider as I stumble back. She shoves me and I go down like a statue, sprawling onto the floor.

"This is almost too easy," she giggles as she steps beside me and looks to Stella. "Well, are you going to help your boyfriend and complete the bet, or-"

I kick her knees in and she crumples onto the floor. I hop up and stare down at her. She, surprisingly, recovers quickly. She comes in close for a jab to the gut. I somehow manage to dodge it, but then she throws a roundhouse kick toward my right ear. It lands true, and I drop to my knees, clutching the side of my head.

"Surprising," she says. "If I weren't in karate, you might have beat me. The games are over. Stop stalling, both of you."

I look at Stella from the ground. Her face is worried, but then is suddenly struck with resolution. She looks at Elsie. "How do I go about this?"

"It's your boyfriend, you decide."

Stella looks back at me. I wonder what I must look like to her. Probably not all that impressive. I just charged someone with full confidence and they knocked me to the floor. On the ground staring up at her, my hands covering my ear. If this were a sitcom, there would be a laughing track playing right now.

"Z." Stella gulps. "I...I'm sorry, but...if I can't..." She seems to be struggling for words, something she doesn't usually do. She speaks what's on her mind all the time, and she does it in a way that you know exactly what she means by it. But now, she fumbles, her eyes darting between me and Elsie. She takes a shaky breath. "Zain Montes, I don't want to be your friend. I don't love you, and I never will."

Something about the way she says it makes me almost believe her. Almost. "You're just saying that," I deny.

"No, I'm not." She seems angry all of a sudden. "I hate you. I hate you not because you're annoying, but because you're just like everyone else. You think you can waltz into my life, lead me on, make me miserable, and then leave without a second thought. Everyone leaves eventually, Zain. Some just take longer than others. Maybe it's time I leave you before you leave me."

Zain. Not Z.

I stare at her. Really look at her. The look on her face, the tone of her voice, the fact there was not a single time she hesitated, told me that she actually believed this. That she actually hated me.

Everyone leaves eventually...Maybe it's time I leave you.

Tears spring to my eyes. I quickly blink them away. No, she's just saying that. She doesn't actually hate me. She's just saying that.

I repeat it to myself over and over until I believe it. A sad look is still on my face, so Elsie thinks differently.

Is that truly what she believes? That everyone leaves her? That no one stays forever?

No.

I would stay.

No matter what happens, I would prove her wrong.

I was not going to leave Estelle Booker.

I was not going to give up on her.

I slump down farther, my hands dropping from my still-ringing ear. "So, what does this mean?" I ask dejectedly.

"It means we aren't friends," Stella snaps. "It means you need to leave me alone."

Elsie smiles and puts her hands on her hips. "Part one done. Now tell me, Stella, where did you disappear to?"

Stella looks like she wants to slap Elsie across the face, but instead she says, "I was with Z. Me and him went to the alley because Z said he goes there a lot. We talked for a bit, maybe kissed, and then we left. I don't know what happened to your faulty tracker, but that's all we did."

It didn't take much effort for a blush to come to my face. Elsie doesn't seem to buy it, though.

"Please. Spare me." Elsie makes a dramatic 'woe-is-me' gesture. "That tracker was not faulty. You want to know how much I paid for that thing? Way too much. Tell me what happened, and make it convincing this time."

Stella glances at me. I can see the question in her eyes. Should she tell her? I shrug. She looks back at Elsie.

"Fine," she announces. "We went to space."

My stomach drops, but Elsie just gives her a blank look. "I said convincing."

Stella shrugs. "One of those was the truth. You pick which."

Elsie stomps her foot. "I'm getting tired of this, Stella. Tell me. You have a total of ten seconds before I take this to the school."

"Alright, alright fine!" Stella shouts. Her hand slips to her pocket. She pulls her phone out and looks at the screen.

"Put it away," Elsie spits.

"Hold on, I got a text." Stella swipes on her screen a few times.

"Who's it from?" Elsie demands.

"My mom." She puts her phone back in her pocket. "I just need you to go over the situation one more time. I seem to have gotten confused. What do I need to do?""You know damn well what you need to do."

"Humor me."

"Fine. You have already completed one part of our arrangement. Now all you need to tell me is what you were doing yesterday that took my tracker off the map. Don't try to stall, just tell me."

"Why, exactly, are we at the school again?"

"Did you not listen to anything I said or are you too stupid to understand it? I'll spell it out for you. Cameras. I know somebody, my brother's friend Mark, who works patrol at night. All I have to do is ask him for the camera footage and it's mine. Blackmail, Stella. I'm blackmailing you. I will go to the school with the camera evidence if you don't do what I ask."

I catch on to what's happening and present my own question. "But, you'll be on the camera evidence too?"

"EDITING." Elsie screams. "I can edit the footage. Show the parts with just you two. Now can we please stop with the questions and get this over with?!"

I can feel a pebble in my shoe. I slip my fingers into my shoe and grope for it. I finally get it and slip my hand free. Stella sees what I'm doing and plays along.

"Elsie!" Stella shouts. "Behind you!"

I throw the pebble for extra effect. It bounces off the floor and into some lockers, creating a tinkling sound that sounds an awful lot like a keychain. Elsie spins around so fast I get whiplash watching her.

I take the opening and scramble up to my feet. I bolt down the hallway, Stella close behind.

"Hey!" Elsie yells, scrambling after us. "This doesn't change anything! I still have evidence!"

Instead of responding, we just run faster. We're going down the stairs, about three at a time, and sprinting through hallways until we get to the main entrance. We burst through the entrance, panting as I pull Stella down the street. A car almost runs into us at an intersection, and that just makes us more on edge as we finally get to our alley, doubling over and breathing heavily.

"As soon as I get home," Stella groans, "I'm burning that sweater."

Then she bursts into tears.

CHAPTER 21

A week after our incident with the Imps, the TU Crew is making headlines. Well, not specifically headlines with TU Crew on it, since they don't know our group name. All the public knows is that a new undercover Hunter crew is out, well, two, for that matter, and on the same day. Not only was the whole school talking about it, but so was the whole United States. New Hunter groups barely ever come, especially not one who doesn't finish their job. And especially not two in one day.

After we high-tailed it out of the apartment, more Imps came in with full force. A new Hunter group had to come and take care of it, and that new Hunter group just so happened to be Mikaya and Ro. They, of course, did their job perfectly and viciously. They exited the apartment to the cheers of onlookers and news reporters, wanting to know who they were and how only two people did the job so effortlessly when four ran away at the first sign of danger. To the first question they answered that their group name was Double Trouble (surprisingly not done yet), and to the second question they didn't respond.

Of course they rubbed it in our faces relentlessly when we got back, and in response I made my team train doubly as hard. They all, of course, complained.

The Councilors told us that we, surprisingly, weren't lying, and that they determined it 'safe until further notice' for us to take new assignments. I assume if something bad happened to us we wouldn't be Hunters anymore, which seems pretty unfair.

The Shedim class was surprisingly terrifying. The Shedim is an ugly, gray creature that reminded me of a mini T-Rex, with an arched back and a long tail, except its back is spiked. It also has razor sharp teeth and a disgustingly long tongue. Its ears are human-like and pointed and its horns are bent at an angle that makes me want to curl in a ball and cry. It has a grand total of four arms. There are even reports of a Shedim's eyes glowing in the dark, apparently as a self defense mechanism. Sort of like a flashbang.

We were sitting in class, staring at professor MacDaniel as he described the Shedim's armored back with spikes, and how we couldn't get a bullet to penetrate it, when Alexander came through the door.

"TU Crew, do you have enough information for a Shedim assignment yet?"

We hop off of our portal at Las Vegas in the middle of an alley. The time zone is three hours before ours, making it about one pm. I hope and pray that we have enough information and training to get this done quickly, and that the Lucifer guy doesn't show up again. The address takes us to a casino/hotel that seems to have been quickly abandoned. A few of the lights are busted out and there is no one around. The gold print above the door reads "The Bicycle Hotel and Casino" with a shield logo between the phrases. There is a hotel complex swirling around the right side of the casino, rising into the sky. The surrounding area has many palm trees and I find it hard to breathe through the humid air outside.

I briskly walk to the entrance and shove the double doors open. A blast of air conditioning smacks me in the face, surprisingly still working. The main area has a lobby with a fountain in the middle. To the back is the entrance to the casino and to the right is the entrance to the hotel. There's an abandoned receptionist desk toward the back wall.

"Maybe we should split up?" Stella asks.

"No, too dangerous," Z answers quickly. "These things could be anywhere, plus they're a lot more dangerous than Imps. If we split up we'll be easier to pick off with no experience."

Again, I am reminded of the fact that they must have shared a moment somewhere between our Imp assignment and our classes this week. Just yesterday, right after class, Z noticed when Stella was feeling down. He asked her what was wrong, and it turned out that she hadn't done well in her auditions for her choir. Z cheered her up by cracking a few jokes, assuring her that she would do better next time, and offered her what little assistance he could.

Neither me nor Rain had noticed until Z had pointed it out, and I doubt we would have if he didn't. Now they are starting to finish each other's thoughts.

"Let's look through the hotel first," Z says. "I have a feeling that the Shedims will be easier to kill if we're confident we can't be snuck up on."

"Can't they sneak up on us from the casino too?" I ask.

"Yeah, I guess," Z mumbles.

"I think we should go to the hotel too," Rain says. "If nothing else, we could leave the easiest place to search for last. I don't think they'd be hiding in an open-floor casino, right?"

"Right," Stella says.

"Let's go, then," I say reluctantly.

We work slowly and tediously, starting with the pool outside. The pool is clean and pretty, with lawn chairs and crystal blue water. I almost want to jump in it. Then we move to the first floor and go through each room and elevator, which are surprisingly working, searching in every nook and cranny. The rooms themselves are very fancy and expensive, with big, plush beds, wide-screen TVs, and pristine bathrooms. We go through each floor until we get to the top, sixth floor. We're tired and bored as we get out of the elevator, only to be met with complete darkness.

I groan as I get a sense of deja vu. Something isn't right on this floor, and I have a feeling we're going to find out what it is soon. Instead of cowering in fear, which I kind of want to do, I step out of the elevator and flip on the night vision on my helmet. I somehow forgot about it the first encounter with Imps and was kind of groping about in the darkness. I make sure to remind my team of our helmets' capabilities now. I also remember the Phor that Alexander made us bring this time. As much as I insisted we wouldn't need it, he told me that we couldn't be too careful.

I shake myself from my thoughts as I creep toward the first door. It pushes open easily and I check the room. Nothing. We repeat this process until the whole floor is clear.

"Weird," Rain muses. "I would have expected-"

She jerks her head to the right and stares. I look from her to the spot she's looking at.

"Rain, what is it-" I suddenly see it too. A dark form in the corner of the hallway. I draw my gun from my holster and face the figure.

Stella and Z are the last ones to notice, just like last time, and just like last time, we are in a living quarters. The deja vu intensifies as the figure emerges from the darkness. A familiar shape appears.

"So we meet again, TU Crew," Lucifer says in his cold voice. "A stupid name, if I may add."

"It is not stupid!" Z shouts.

"Seriously?" he scoffs. "What does it even stand for?"

A silence.

"Teens Undercover," Z mumbles.

Lucifer laughs out loud at this. "See? Stupid."

"Whatever, what are you doing here?" Rain quips.

"To torment you, of course, until you join me." He smiles. "This could get rather repetitive quickly and, whether you think you will or not, you're going to just keep coming back until you join me. Trust me, I used See on it. Now right now I realize that you have no regard toward yourselves, you did come here blindly, after all. But you might have regards for others. You might have regards toward innocent human lives."

"What are you talking about?" Stella ventures, her voice shaky.

"I'm talking about the fact that all the Shedims are in the casino right now, waiting for my command to break down the doors and enter the city, free to tear humans apart, humans who have no training and no experience. Not to mention absolutely no weapons that effectively hurt Shedims. Oh, plus, a Ghost Ghoul ready to enter the city and possess someone."

I swallow hard. I remember the Ghouls from the demon and ghost sheet. Demon versions of ghouls are basically zombies, eating flesh from dead people and alive people if they can get to them. Ghost Ghouls behave as actual ghosts, though. They don't really feed on flesh, but they can possess people, like every other ghost.

If Lucifer isn't bluffing, and there really are Shedims and a ghost to take care of, we would have to split up into two groups, maybe even three for Lucifer. I decide that two people who work together best would be good for the Shedims, which would surprisingly be Stella and Z, and two people, me and Rain, would go after the Ghost Ghoul in case of emergencies.

"So, let's say you aren't bluffing," I say, my mind working fast. "Where would that leave you? What are you doing while we take care of this?"

"Watching, of course," he states, looking offended I would even ask. "I don't usually get my hands dirty, I leave that to my minions."

"Okay, then," I say. "See you next time, I guess."

I bolt toward the elevator, dragging my friends behind me. We enter the elevator and set it for the ground floor. As we head toward the lobby, I tell them the plan.

"Alright, Rain, you're with me. I have a Phor to catch the Ghoul. Stella and Z, you're going after the Shedims. If anything, anything, goes wrong, fall back and wait for me and Rain to get back to help. Have one of your helmets showing what we see so we know if anything goes wrong, and we'll do the same for you. Remember that citizen lives are at risk, we have absolutely zero room for error."

"Good luck out there," Z says to me and Rain when we reach the lobby.

"You too." I turn on Z and Stella's vision on my helmet and make them smaller off to the side. I nod at Rain and we run for the main entrance doors.

"Where do you think this thing is?" she asks once we get outside. I flip on a special vision for seeking ghosts on my helmet.

"I guess we just search around some graveyards or something," I look around the outside of the resort. There are no ghostly presences. "I wish I would have asked him where the Ghoul even was."

"I think I remember seeing a graveyard on our way here. Should we check that out?"

"Couldn't hurt," I say to her, following as she runs down the street.

The graveyard is exactly what I expected it to be: terrifying. The Phor is gripped in my hand as we traverse through gravestones and trees, the abrupt fog making it almost impossible to see. Based on Stella and Z's screens, it seems they are doing well. There's a lot more Shedims than I expected, but they fend them off every time. Shedims are surprisingly slow, and even though some are friendly, this group is definitely not. There were a few close calls that had me tensing and stopping to see the result, but they handled it like pros.

I shake back to the present and scan the graveyard again. Nothing. Stella and Z being in the middle of battle makes me on edge. I want this to be over with so I can help them.

"Look!" Rain whispers. She points toward an old gravestone that has an angel perched on top. The name reads 'Elizabeth Caty Polt: 1898-1935, a wife, mother, sister, and daughter.' Standing above it is a ghost that faintly resembles a little girl, staring up at the angel with a sad look on her face. She looks over to a grave next to it, this one smaller. 'Mary Grace Polt: 1930-1937, taken too soon.' She goes back to staring at the mossy angel above the headstone.

"It looks like it's just a little kid," I mumble. "Maybe we can sneak up behind her. It can't cause much harm, right?"

I take a step forward. The girl's head slowly turns toward me. My breath catches in my throat. The little girl tilts her head and turns toward me fully. I study her for a second. She has a nightdress on, a teddy bear clutched in her hand, and blood running down her chin and onto her gown. She looks hopeful for a second, and then terrified, and then angry.

The girl moves toward us. I can't move, frozen in place. Rain pushes me, but it has no effect. The little girl is almost to me now. Rain shoves me again, trying to pull me away. My feet are grounded to the earth, but all I can do is look into the girl's sad, terrified, angry eyes as her ghostly self enters my body.

I drop to the dirty, cold ground, convulsing. Rain drops beside me immediately and takes off my helmet, grabbing my face.

"Milo!" she shouts. "Milo, wake up!"

I know what's happening to me, I'm being possessed, so I shove the Toph into her hands quickly, my hands barely able to hold it. A force moves through my body and up my throat. I realize with a start that this force is my soul. I'm dying. If Rain doesn't get me back to the Academy quickly, I might stay dead forever.

Rain starts to sob. The last thing I hear is a voice that is not my own speak through me.

"Milo is not here anymore."

CHAPTER 22

"Milo is not here anymore."

Milo says this, but it is not his voice that speaks, but a little girls'. Nor is it his eyes that look at me from the ground with so much pain that I can barely breathe, frozen in place. These eyes are glowing, a ghostly gray color.

"Who?" I sob, scrambling away from Milo. "Who are you?"

"My name is Mary Grace Polt. I was born in 1930 and I died in 1936. That's what they told me, anyway. I don't know how I died, but I was really cold, and I was really hurt. I miss my mama and my papa. Have you seen them anywhere?"

She says these things quickly, like a child does. She's standing now, almost falling from being in a new body, I assume. I think, based on what her ghost form looked like, that she died from a lung disease, maybe Tuberculosis? Did they have a cure for that in the 1930s? "What are your parents' names?"

"My mama's named Elizabeth, and my papa's name is Christopher. I saw mama's name over there on that stone, so I thought she would be around here. My name's right next to hers. On that other stone."

I realized, suddenly, that Mary had been here since she died, looking for her parents. 1936 was more than 100 years ago. More than a century.

"Your parents must be really worried. I have a question, though, Mary. Why are you in my friend?"

Milo's face looks guilty. "I'm sorry, I had to find a way to speak with you.""It's alright," I say quickly. "It's just, if you stay in there too long, he could die. I would really like for my friend not to die, please."

Mary nodded but then stopped. "I don't like your machine. It's scary."

"Oh, this?" I place the Phor on the ground. "I'm sorry, it's okay. I won't hurt you. But, Mary, this machine will take you to your mama and papa. Would you like that?"

She shifts. "Mama told me to not trust strangers."

"I know, Mary, but I really need you to get out of Milo."

"I do not think my mama and papa would like you. You dress wacky. You should be wearing a dress, not pants. You'll get mistaken for a boy!"

"Mary, please." I start to cry again. "Just get out of him." I turn to Stella and Z's vision. They look like they're done with the Shedims. They're outside of the hotel, so I connect my audio and location to them. All I can do is hope they get here soon.

"I won't. I don't want to fight you, strange girl, because that would be unlady-like, but I'm a boy now, so I will if I have to."

She stumbles toward me. I don't know much about possessions, or fighting, for that matter, but I know I can't hurt Milo. I just have to subdue him long enough to get him to the academy. They would know what to do, right?

I sidestep her and push her to the floor. She falls ungracefully to the ground.

Mary doesn't have enough control over Milo, and she's spiritually only six years old, so she knows a lot less about fighting than I do, but she still has Milo's body. And Milo knows karate. He's also really good at it, so we might be on the same skill level.

She seems to have enough control over Milo, because she's kneeling on the ground and lunging at me before I can understand what she's doing. She wraps her arms around me and shoves me to the ground. My head smacks the ground and she punches my stomach in a very wrong form. The breath is, still, knocked out of me. She winces at her hand, but wraps it and her other one around my throat and I choke.

My hand slithers to my holster, where I got a knife from Alexander. I can't kill Milo, but I can slow Mary down. I'm sure Milo wouldn't mind a scratch if it meant saving his life. I grab my knife and slash it across Mary/Milo's forearm. Blood seeps from the wound immediately. Mary pulls back with a grimace as she clutches her arm.

I punch her in the face, and Mary gets knocked out. I wince at the already-forming bruise right on Milo's cheek. I stare down at her as I catch my breath and take my helmet off. I rip off a piece of my uniform and wrap it around Milo's arm.

That's the time Stella and Z decide to join the fight. They leap into the clearing and shout until they see me, knelt over him. I can't imagine how I look.

"Help me," I whimper.

We got to the Launch Pad and brought him inside. I had no idea how scary death could be until that moment. Until I was willing to fight a scared little girl in order to get him back. Until I was running to Alexander so fast I'm pretty sure I set a record. Until he was on a metal table in an infirmary room filled with candles. The Councilors are in the room with us, surrounding him. We all are surrounding him, including Alexander, staring at his body on the table.

"We are going to exorcize him," Atara says, "and then bring his soul back. It won't be a pretty sight. I'd never wish seeing a loved one exorcized on my worst enemy. You don't have to be here, the ritual works with three people."

"I'm not leaving him," I say firmly.

"Neither are we," Z says.

Atara sighs. "Fine. But don't say I didn't warn you."

We all join hands above Milo. The Councilors close their eyes. Atara starts chanting in a language I don't recognize, something old and halting, clipped. The candles start burning brighter, hotter, and pretty soon it seems like we're in an inferno.

The other councilors start chanting, too. At this point, Milo is lifted into the air, fire surrounding the air around him. A gray wind is surrounding us, swirling underneath him. His eyes and mouth fly open, glowing with the same color as the wind. The same ghostly color his eyes were in the graveyard. He starts convulsing in the air, the same movement he made when Mary took control of him.

I clutch the Phor in my hand, ready to use it as soon as Mary leaves Milo's body. The Phor is just a box with a button in the middle. Easy enough. Get close enough to capture her.

A high pitched scream from a girl splits the room as the chanting builds to a crescendo. The circle starts to float, too. The feeling of weightlessness comes to me. How insignificant I am, compared to this moment. Compared to the world. Compared to the universe. I'm just a star in the galaxy, a grain of sand on the beach, a drop of water in the vast, blue ocean. Tears stream down my cheeks and all at once, the fire goes out. The chanting and the scream stops.

A silence so heavy it feels that the weight of the world is on my shoulders.

I see a gray, wispy shape leave Milo's body and another one, glowing brighter, goes through his still-open mouth and into his body. He drops to the table with a clang. We stop floating and the force of gravity hits me with full force. I drop to the floor, landing on my ankle in an odd way. I wince and watch as the gray wispy shape takes the form of Mary. Just a little girl, clutching a teddy bear, looking scared out of her mind.

I limp toward her. "Mary."

Her head turns to me. "Please. I just want my parents."

I press the button on the Phor. She tries to scramble away, but she doesn't get very far. The Phor is taking her spirit, guiding it to heaven.

"I'm scared," she whispers, fading away.

"I know," I say. "You'll see them soon, I swear. I swear. I swear."

I keep repeating it until she's gone. I drop to the floor and stare at the Phor.

"I'm sorry, Mary Polt."

I stayed in the infirmary with Milo the rest of the afternoon. That is, for thirty minutes, for he had to be taken to an actual hospital. The Academy had to call his parents and tell them that he got hurt during school and he passed out. He was going to be admitted into a hospital in Pittsburgh. I wondered what their phone's area code would be in space, and how they even got service up here, but didn't dwell on it too long. The Councilors told us that the doctors wouldn't be that suspicious since he got his soul back after the exorcism, but it would still take him a few days to recover. They told us to head home afterward.

I couldn't. I had to make sure he was okay, so I went with them when they took him to the emergency room. I helped them carry

Milo through the portal and into an unmarked van. They put him in the far back, on the floor. I stayed with him and realized that this van would be a Hunter van without a logo. Despite everything, I smiled. I imagined myself driving this van to an assignment, except I wouldn't be driving since I don't even have a driver's license.

The emergency room was glaringly white and made me want to throw up. I stayed by his side until I physically couldn't anymore, until the doctors told me to leave, and that only family could stay. I said I was his sister, but they didn't believe me. Now, I'm walking to my house in the cold. It's around eight, I just checked my phone and found ten unanswered texts from my parents and two missed calls. I sent them a brief text back about being on my way. I prepared for the worst as I trudged my way back home.

I enter my house and the first thing I see is Beanie running toward me. I want to cry at the familiar sight as she jumps up on me. I pet her and throw my bag on the ground.

"Rain?" I can hear my mom move toward me. She can tell something is up. I stare at her as she comes over to me.

"What's wrong, baby?" she asks, wrapping me in a hug.

"My friend, Milo, he..." I choke on a knot in my throat. "I can't..." She pulls back and looks at me.

I drop to the floor by my golden retriever and sob. Great, heaving sobs that rack my body. I bury my face into Beanie's fluffy fur. Mom kneels beside me and wraps her arms around me.

Everything that has happened over the two weeks, being a Hunter, being in perilous danger, having lives in my hands, Milo, poor little Mary, it all catches up to me. I pray to whoever is in the sky that Mary finds her parents, that Milo makes it out okay, and that I survive whatever is going to happen to me next.

I can be strong later. Right now, I think, I can cry.

CHAPTER 23

Milo didn't get better for a week. Rain, of course, was worried sick the whole time. Every second she wasn't training or in school was spent in the hospital by Milo's side. She told Z and I that she bumped into his parents a few times on the way to see him. She eventually found out that if she acted like she was her girlfriend she could see him. When he finally did wake up, Rain's face was the first one he saw. He was now back at the Academy, but he was kind of slow on his feet and looked sickly.

I knew there was some sense of poeticness in this, but I didn't want to dwell on it too long because I have had my own problems. Elsie went to the school with the evidence. They called me and Z down during fifth period on Monday and had us explain ourselves. I showed them the recording I had on my phone.

They contacted Elsie and Mark and sent them into the office with us. Mark, a scruffy man who looked like a drug dealer, admitted to it, but Elsie wouldn't be moved.

"That could be forged!" Elsie had shouted. "I need video proof too."

That was apparently the wrong thing to say, because Mark pulled up the actual footage and showed Elsie there too. In the end, Z and I got a week's worth of, thankfully, lunch detention, but it could have been a lot worse. Elsie got suspended for a few days.

I didn't converse with my old group of friends after that and let them draw their own conclusions. I now sit with my Hunter friends at lunch and hope I won't get used by them too.

Now I am heading to the Training Wing with my group. We got called by Carlos and Tony. Once we get there they usher us inside. Alexander is here too.

"What are we doing up here?" Milo asks.

"Well," Carlos states, "the Councilors decided that a group exercise could be good for you guys in this situation. After a careful analysis of what happened that day using See, we've decided that communication is not the best between you guys, and that Milo's possession could have been prevented with it. You all must trust each other with everything. So, today, we are going to be doing a trust exercise.

"The premise is simple, the simulation we give you taps into your brain and finds your biggest fear. You're phobia, so to speak. We will be projecting what happens onto the big screen up on the wall. Your job is to get through your phobia and to have enough faith in your friends that you trust them with that fear and weakness. Maybe we could do another exercise like this but with your weakness, or your strengths. Today we're starting slow with a phobia."

A rock drops in my stomach. Starting slow? This is so much worse than the simulations with the Imps and Shedims. In those simulations, we all went at the same time, so we can't see exactly what happens. Plus with those, we're facing a rational thing we're prepared for. I don't even know what my greatest fear is, it might not even be a palpable thing, like a spider. It could be something psychological.

"I'll go first," Rain mumbles. "Better to get it over with."

They strap her to the machine and she lays on the table. What she is seeing is projected onto the screen, and it's nothing but black.

"It says here she has two fears," Tony mumbles. "It doesn't show me what they are until we get through them. First one it is, then."

A click is heard from his computer. The screen slowly fades into a blank room. She looks around. The walls are blank, the floor is blank, even the ceiling. Just plain white.

She goes to the far end of the room and places her hand on the wall. Is this really her fear? A white room?

My mind is running through the why until the white slowly fades to gray. The walls almost seem to be moving inward. That's when I realize that they are moving inward. She scrambles back to the middle of the room. She looks up and I see that the ceiling is moving inward too. She starts hyperventilating and crouches low to the floor. The walls and ceiling are pressing into her completely now, and she's smooshed down into a ball. I can hear her erratic heartbeat through the speakers on the TV.

Confined spaces. That's her first fear. A rational fear, I realize. The walls are fading from gray to black now, and she has to have her forehead to her knees. Suddenly she stops moving and starts taking really deep breaths. The walls ever so slowly start giving her some more room, brightening to a lighter color, until they get back to the original state of the room. The word "conquered" appears at the bottom of the screen.

"Claustrophobia," Tony says. "The fear of confined spaces."

The screen fades to black and Rain sits up. She shoves the headset off. "Am I done?"

"Not yet," Carlos says. "You've got one more big fear."

She heaves a sigh and slips the headset back on, lowering herself to the table. Another click comes from Tony's computer.

The screen fades to a door on the outside of a house. Rain seems to recognize the house, because she gets a key from under the mat and opens the door, stepping inside.

The layout of a house comes into view, what seems to be a mudroom and a staircase farther forward. To the right is a kitchen and farther forward is a living room. She throws her bag to the ground and walks forward, but then she stops. Listens.

"Beanie?" she asks, stepping forward. "Where are you?"

No response. She goes to the kitchen and looks around. She searches the living room as well. There doesn't seem to be anyone around down here, so she goes upstairs.

The hallway has a few doors here and there. She opens the one farthest down the hall. It's a master bedroom with a bathroom connected to it. She frowns and pulls out her phone. There are no new messages.

She searches the whole upstairs and finds no one. She frantically runs down the stairs and searches again. She goes to the backyard and finds no one out there. She finds nothing.

At this point, Rain starts freaking out. She searches the house a couple of times. She calls her mom and dad about a hundred times, they don't answer, until finally a knock sounds at the door.

She bolts toward it and swings it open, probably expecting her parents.

What she finds instead is a police officer staring at her. His hat is off and his face is blurred.

"Are you Rain Farley?" he asks.

"Yes," she answers warily. "Do you know where my parents are?"

"I'm so very sorry to inform you of this, but you're parents and your dog got into a devastating car crash."

Rain's breathing somehow becomes even more erratic. "Are they okay?"

"None of them made it out alive."

Rain crumples to the floor. Drops. She buries her head in her hands and sobs. She sounds a lot like she's dying.

"Do you have anyone else you can live with?"

This seems to make Rain cry impossibly harder, but she shakes her head and somehow gets up. The police officer gestures to his car, and she goes with him to his police car. A green "conquered" shows up at the bottom of the screen.

"Thanatophobia," Carlos whispers. "The fear of yourself or people you love dying."

Rain sits up straight and yanks her headset off. She is crying. We watch her as she gets off the table and straightens.

"Are you okay?" Milo asks, moving toward her and pulling her into a hug.

"No," she pulls away, "but it was just a simulation, right? I'll be fine."

She wipes her tears and goes to the wall, leaning against it heavily.

It suddenly makes sense to me why she was so obsessive over making sure Milo was okay. That meant he was a loved one to her. Was Stella considered a loved one?

Milo steps up next. "I'll go."

He was strapped to the machine. He puts the headset on, and lays onto the table.

A click sounds from Tony's keyboard and the simulation shows up on the screen. The setting is in a classroom, and Milo is sitting in the front row, right in the middle.

A teacher is handing back graded tests. Some writing on the board says 'Final grade! No retakes!' The teacher is smiling at everybody, all of them with a big red A on the paper. His smile fades as he looks at the next sheet and places it face-down on Milo's desk.

"Not your best work," the teacher scolds, a frown coming over his face. "Come see me after class."

Milo has tears in his eyes and he flips over the sheet, seeing a big F at the top. The kids around him exclaim how easy the test was, then they move on to different subjects, like 'did you see that big game yesterday?' 'I hope my mom isn't mad at me when I get home' and one that makes Milo freeze.

'Did you see how bad that last hunter group was? And with four people? What a rip off, I could totally become a Hunter.'

Stella knew that the kids were just talking to talk, but Milo didn't seem to realize this. He shoves the paper into his bag and takes a deep breath as the bell rings. Everyone files out of the classroom, and a green 'conquered' shows up at the bottom of the screen.

"Atychiphobia," Tony says. "Fear of failure."

It suddenly all makes sense to me. Why he didn't want to quit the assignments, why he's been making us train a lot harder, why he gets absolutely perfect grades in every subject. Why he looks so tired all the time.

Milo sits up really slowly and takes his headset off with care. He doesn't say a word as he goes to stand by Rain.

Z is up next, sliding onto the table with a frown on his face. He plucks the headset off the metal and puts it on.

Another click sounds and a room shows up before Z. It looks like a kitchen, with an old, yellowing backsplash and beaten up appliances. A woman with blonde hair is standing at the sink, leaning against it heavily.

"I just don't know what to do, Z." The woman starts to cry. Z makes no move to help her. He just watches as she slumps to the floor. "I just don't know what to do."

"Yes, you do," Z's voice is cold, unlike how I've ever heard it. "You know exactly what to do, you're just too scared to do anything about it. Divorce him. Step in sometimes. You can do so many things, but you're too much of a coward to do any of that!" He's shouting now.

Suddenly a door bangs open. Z looks past the kitchen arch. The living room, which he's looking into, is basic and foreboding. Something about it, maybe the worn in La-Z-Boy recliner, maybe the stains on the walls and ceilings, maybe the beer cans everywhere, makes it terrifying.

A big, beer-bellied man with graying hair stomps into the room, stumbling a bit like a drunk man. He wears a tank top with stains and jean shorts. His face is cruel.

Z seems to make himself smaller. He speed- walks over to the staircase, which is in the back of the house, but the man yells at him to stop. He turns around slowly, staring at the floor.

"What did you do to your mother?" he asks angrily. He points to the blonde woman crumpled dejectedly by the sink.

"Nothing, sir," Z mumbles.

"What was that?" he bellows.

"Nothing, sir," Z says, louder this time.

"Liar!" he screams, stomping his foot. "Why is she on the floor then?"

"She was just looking for something she drop- ped, right, mom?" Z looks back at her.

The woman, Z's mom, stares down at the kitchen tiles, about to cry. She says nothing for Z's defense, just shrinks in on herself more.

The man, Z's father, looks back at him. "Zain, would you apologize to your mother for what you did to her?"

"Don't call me that," Z says.

"Your name? Do you want me to call you by your preferred name, Z?"

Z nods.

"What was that?"

"Yes, sir," Z says.

Z's father backhands him across the face. He stumbles back.

"I will use the name I gave you!" Z's father roars. "Stop complaining, you ungrateful brat! You can barely pass your classes, what makes you think you have the authority over me?"

The screen suddenly takes on a darker color around the edges. Z straightens up and looks to his mom, who is staring at her son with horror. Z seems to get a resolution, because he pushes past his father, much to his dismay, and sprints out the front door. As he bolts down the street, a green 'conquered' shows up at the bottom of the screen.

"Patrophobia," Carlos says in shock. "The fear of one's father."

Z sits upright quickly, panting. He takes off his headset and stares at us. We stare at him.

Alexander steps forward. "Z, if you're having struggles at home, we can always contact CPS and-"

"No!" Z blurts. He pauses. "I mean, that barely ever happens. Like, ever. He's gotten better, I swear. He doesn't hit me, and my mom's even thinking of divorcing him. It's all fine!"

None of them seem convinced, but Alexander nods anyway. Z gets off the table and staggers over to the wall where Rain and Milo are waiting.

I realize then that no one else is before me. My heart hammers in my chest as I step to the table and sit on it. I take a deep breath and prepare for the very worst as I slip on the headset.

A click resounds like a final heartbeat. That's the last thing I hear as I'm thrown into a simulation.

I take in my surroundings quickly. For some reason, I don't remember getting here.

I'm in the Training wing at the Academy, near the main entrance. My friends told me to meet them by the staircase on the second floor. I even pull out my phone for a text from Milo to confirm my thoughts. I trudge toward the staircase and up the stairs. The Academy looks oddly bright today, sort of like if I was in a dream. I shrug it off as I climb the staircase at a slow pace.

By the time I get to the top I have a feeling something is wrong. Very wrong. I see my friends there, staring at me with equal looks of resentment, like I did something unforgivable. Nerves immediately settled in my stomach. What did you do this time, Stella?

I approach them warily. They don't speak for a minute, just staring at me.

"So, why did you guys call me here?" I shift my stance. "Is there an assignment or something?"

"No, Stella," Z says. "There won't be any more assignments for you."

My stomach sinks. They couldn't possibly mean... "What are you talking about?"

"We're kicking you out of our group, Stella," Rain crosses her arms. "I can't believe you would do something like that."

I stare. I stare and stare at them.

"What?"

"Don't play dumb," Milo accuses. "You know exactly how you fooled the Councilors into thinking you were any good. You can barely catch an Imp! We're better off without you."

I stare and stare some more. I can't believe this.

"So, that's it?" I ask, so scared. "After everything, you just...leave me?"

"You can go ask Alexander if you can join a separate team," Z mumbles, "but you're not staying with us. Go away. No one wants you here."

I suddenly remember that this is a simulation, that my real friends are watching me right now, watching what choice I make. If I want to get back, I have to leave.

"Oh," I step back. "Okay, then."I turn around and race back down the stairs. This felt oddly real, and I realize this could happen to me at any time. That's when I realize that none of these simulations were really fake, these could all happen at any time, and we have no control to leave the simulation when that time comes. A green 'conquered' appears at the bottom of my vision. The simulation fades away.

"Autophobia," Tony says. "Fear of being alone or abandoned."

I sit up and take the headset off. I look at my friends' equally shocked faces. I can't take this. This is a whole new level of embarrassment and fear. I hop off the table and shove the door open, bolting down the hallway and to the staircase. I take the steps two at a time up the stairs and burst through the door leading to a balcony on the third floor. I get to the edge and stop in my tracks, plopping down onto the floor and starting to cry, my head buried in my hands.

I think about my future, and how no matter how hard I try, I might not be good enough. My friends might kick me off the team. My friends' fears occur to me and I realize that mine are silly. Being abandoned is much easier than being dead, or having someone you love die. Being abandoned is much better than having an abusive father and a mother that just watches. Being abandoned is much better than failing when you should be good at something.

As I sob over how stupidly scared I am, I hear the door open. Alexander sits next to me in silence, looking out over the galaxy.

Something about his presence calms me down. I stop crying and look out, too.

Compared to the universe, my problems are so tiny. This just makes me want to cry harder, but Alexander opens his mouth.

"You know, your friends would never say that," he says matter-of-factly. "I might not notice much, but I notice how important you are to each other. I notice how much they care because they immediately wanted to follow you up here, but I told them to let me go up and talk to you.

"That being said, I also know how much they count on you to do your best, but, Stella, the whole reason we set this up wasn't to humiliate you all, it was to get you to rely on each other. I realize now why that could be hard for you, and why you don't rely on people much, or even let them rely on you, but you have to trust them. They trust you to try."

"I know, Alexander, but I'm so scared." I swallow hard and look at him.

"Stella, fears are a way for your mind to let you know something isn't safe, but sometimes you have to listen to your heart." He stops talking and keeps on staring off.

"Do you remember that day on your Imp assignment last week? Do you remember how I pulled you aside and told you that if you didn't talk to them, if you didn't trust them, you wouldn't get far?"

I nod, not quite knowing where this is going.

"You've grown a lot in the span of that week, Stella. I can tell that you actually want to try now."

I look at him and then back out at the inky abyss of space. Then I remember something.

"That first day, in the attic, I was about to leave, but you didn't stop me. You let me figure out the decision on my own. Did you know, then, that I'd join anyway?"

"Honestly, no, I didn't." He turns to look at me. "A small part of me thought you were actually just going to leave, but another part of me had faith that you wouldn't. I think a part of me could already tell how amazing you guys would be together, how much you guys could change the world.

"You know, Stella, you remind me of a baby bird. You're so scared to spread your wings, but you have so much potential. You can soar above the world and see everything there is to see. You can be brave and take on any wind or storm you face, but you just have to take that first leap."

I stare at him. "But what if I fall?"

"But what if you fly?"

When I travel back down the stairs, I think about what's going to happen next. What challenges faced me, and would I be able to bear them? Could I save my friends and everyone I loved most?

I open the door to the Simulation room and my friends immediately bombard me with a huge hug.

"I'm so sorry," Z tells me. "We're sorry for giving you any doubts that we don't want you as a friend, Stella. You're the best, most cool person I've met, and anyone would be lucky to have you as a friend."

"Exactly!" Rain shouts, a bit loudly. She winces and lowers her voice. "Sorry. But, Z's right. We would never, ever do that, and you don't need to feel embarrassed."

"We're also sorry for not coming up to see you right away," Milo chimes in, "but Alexander made some convincing points, and I wasn't even sure you wanted to see us, and-"

"It's okay, guys," Stella interrupts, "if anything, I should be apologizing. I'm sorry for doubting you guys, I'm sorry for not trusting you, and I'm sorry for letting you all down. From here on out, I'm going to be such a good Hunter, you won't even remember how bad I was."

Chapter 24

I'm not sure what happened to Stella after our fear simulation, but she made good on her promise. She started training like an absolute crazy person. I seriously thought that she was going to pass out based on how much information she was taking and how much she trained herself. She was on the same level as Milo by the end of that week. She was also a lot friendlier with everybody. I don't know what Alexander said to her, or what that fear simulation did to her, but it was apparently life changing.

The Councilors had told us that nothing was guaranteed yet. If they deemed it too dangerous, they had to erase our minds and send us on our way. I really didn't want to do that. They also said that since we've already had an experience with a Ghoul, we didn't need to go on a Ghoul assignment or have a Ghoul simulation.

The class we had the next week was Raveners, in the Egyn wing, which meant that our Uniforms got an upgrade from the green colors to the yellow colors. Anyway, Raveners were even more terrifying than Shedims. Most Raveners had these worm-like bodies for the bottom half, and the top half kind of like a human. It reminded me of a mermaid but a lot more ugly. Also, their mouths could literally swallow us whole. They have this special mouth that can basically unhinge and stretch really far. It would be funny and remind me of a cartoon if it wasn't so utterly scary.

The simulation for Raveners was surprisingly easy, since Raveners are actually really slow. We just have to steer clear of their mouths and we should be good. We're waiting for our next assignment in a break room in the training wing when Mikaya and Ro burst into the room.

"Guys!" Ro shouts. "You will not believe what we just found!"

"What is it?" Stella asks, immediately on her feet.

"We still aren't entirely sure," Mikaya confides, "but we wanted to come to you first because you guys would definitely know what it means."

"What?" Rain questions.

"Just follow us," Ro says, turning and rushing out the door, Mikaya on his heels.

I turn to my friends and shrug, following them out.

We end up on the third floor, in front of the Councilor's doors.

"What are we doing here?" Milo wonders.

"Just come on," Mikaya says, motioning to follow her as she goes to the balcony. "The door to the Councilors' room is locked, so we just went to the balcony and found this window outside, so we obviously went inside, and we found this-"

"Wait, you snuck into the Councilors' room?" I blurt. "Dude that sounds like something I would do. No way you guys trespassed."

"We did," Mikaya murmurs. "For good reason, though. Well, we were actually just bored. But we did find this letter, and that's what we wanted to talk to you guys about."

"When, exactly, did you find this letter?" Milo asks, opening the door to the balcony.

"Right before we came to get you," Ro informs, going to the edge of the balcony toward a window. "Now, help me, Mikaya. I can't open this thing by myself."

With a series of boosts and stretching, they somehow open the window enough for someone to slip through. They boost us up and we jump to the window, the slight change of gravity helping us not fall to the ground. Mikaya goes last, and Ro has to grab her out of the air so she makes it inside. There isn't a single Councilor in sight.

"Where are they?" Milo asks.

"Who cares?" I smile. "Now, where was that letter you were talking about?"

Mikaya goes to the Councilors' big table and finds a non-sealed letter sitting there. She picks it up and hands it to us. Milo grabs it and reads it out loud.

Griffin,

I saw you the first day I came here, scared and worried for what was ahead of me, but you were smiling. At first you looked so scary, but there you were, smiling at me. It was the brightest smile I had seen that day, like a light at the end of the tunnel. You told me not to worry, you told me that it was all going to be okay, and I believed you. Of course I believed you. I almost fell in love with you right there on the spot. So, I guess what I'm trying to say is thank you for giving me the brightest smile that day. And thank you for telling me what I needed to hear. I love you.

  -Lottie

We stare at each other for a bit. Lottie and Griffin? The two youngest Councilors, in love? From what this note looks like, it seems to be a secret, but that doesn't mean we couldn't use this to our advantage. Or maybe it was only me thinking that last bit.

"Was this opened when you found it?" Rain asks.

"Yep," Ro says. "I don't know where this Griffin guy went, but it seems to have been abandoned here not that long ago."

"I could take a picture of it," Stella offers. "That way we can still have it but it wouldn't disappear if Griffin comes back."

"Good idea," Rain inputs. Stella pulls out her phone and snaps a picture of the letter and the envelope it came in. She shoves it back in her pocket.

"Alright," Milo says. "We should probably get out of here before Griffin comes-"

We hear footsteps out in the hall, coming straight for the door.

"Hide!" I hiss. Stella rearranges the letter quickly and hops behind the table with us. The table is actually set more like a desk, so people coming in can't see the legs, or, in this case, the people, behind it.

The door swings open. "Yes, I know," a male voice grumbles, venturing towards us. I scoot in more so whoever is in the room can't see my legs. I press my face down to the small space between the bottom of the desk and the floor. A pair of black shoes are there, a shadow being cast toward us.

"I know that, too," the voice mumbles, "but we can't keep lying like this. Not only is the public going to find out soon, but it's also leaving a terrible taste in my mouth. We haven't even tried to contact them and yet we keep attacking-" he stops, like someone cut him off. "I don't see what that has to do with now, though! If we don't stop this...but we can't just...yes, I feel bad, Alexander! Of course I feel bad, and it's sickening you don't either. We can't keep lying to them, and we can't keep lying to our Hunters... Of course I want everyone to be safe, what kind of a question-" He cuts himself off with a sigh. His voice is facing away from us, so I peak out over the top of the desk. Griffin.

"Yeah, alright, bye," Griffin concludes. "We are not done talking about this, though." He, I assume, hangs up the phone and heaves a great sigh. I think we're done for as he comes to our table, but he just grabs the letter Lottie wrote. He stops for a second on his way out and I hold my breath. He walks over to the window and shuts it, then his footsteps exit the room. We slowly disentangle ourselves from under the table and look at each other.

"What was that about?" Mikaya asks.

"I don't know," I mumble, "but we should probably get out of here."

We go to the door and slowly scan the hall to make sure no one is there. Once it's clear, we rush down the stairs as fast as we can while still being quiet. Our group heads toward the break room, shoving open the door and finding spots around the room.

I think about what Griffin said. What did he mean, lying? What were they lying about? Why would the Councilors ever lie? Who are they trying to contact? Why are they attacking them?

I'm about to say something about this when the door to the break room opens and Alexander comes in.

"The Councilors are giving you one last chance. If you make it through this assignment with no bumps, then you all are free to continue being Hunters. Sorry, Ro and Mikaya, this doesn't really apply to you."

"It's fine," Ro says quickly, hauling himself and Mikaya to their feet. "We'll be leaving now." They rush out of the break room at break-neck speed.

"What was that about?" Alexander asks.

"Probably just excited," Milo mumbles.

Or scared.

Of Alexander.

EPILOGUE

I was getting sick of worrying at this point. In between being in simulations for trust exercises, finding Lottie's letter, also finding out that the Councilors are lying about something, and this being the assignment that could make or break everything that we've done so far, I'd say this is a pretty appropriate time to worry.

We got to Seattle, Washington at around five fifteen, but the time zone here made it about two. We found a van waiting for us, an IDHS logo on the side. Alexander warned us ahead of time that there would be, but it still kind of shocked me as we piled in. The interior was the same as the van that was used to carry Milo, but this time I could appreciate it more. Milo was doing the driving, and the rest of us were in the back with the weapons and such.

Now we pull up to the Space Needle parking lot, and a feeling of dread washes over me looking at the towering pillar in the sky. Not only do we have to go up there, but we also have to fight Raveners in there? That high up, and with glass, there was a danger of any of us falling.

I gulp as Milo puts the car in park and opens the door in the front, hopping out. Z presses a button by the van's back and a ramp comes down in the back of the car. We leave the van, stocking up on guns and some new knives that Alexander showed us how to use.

The knives have a certain amount of Goph in them, and a system coats the knife every time it gets dry. Once again, I'm shocked by the mechanics of IDHS, and how they manage to do these things with a single element.

We wander toward the visitors center. There's one person there, standing at the register, a terrified look on her face. She looks to be a teenager, maybe a little bit older than us, with brown hair, brown eyes, and a keycard hanging around her neck.

"I apologize," the girl stammers, "but the Space Needle isn't open at this time, we currently have a situation with some demons. We're waiting for the IDHS to arrive, and-" she notices our van and attire. "You're the Hunter group, right? The new one? With four people?"

"That's us," I answer.

"Thank God!" she exclaims. "Please, come on in!"

"Wait," Milo interrupts. "Did you say 'we'? As in, more than just you?"

The girl looks confused. "Yes, we all evacuated the top viewing deck soon after the first Demon arrived. There shouldn't be any-one up there now, but we shut down the elevators as soon as we left. There were, thankfully, no casualties, and we are all in the lobby."

"Well, why didn't you leave?" Stella asks.

"We didn't want to leave our jobs unattended, we might not get paid for this."

We look at her for a second.

"Does this happen often?" Milo questions.

"No, first time, why?"

"Uhm," Z says warily, "can you give us a second?" He turns to us and lowers his voice. "What do we do? We need to evacuate all civilians, and they don't seem to be leaving."

We regard this.

"I say we just do our thing and leave," I venture. "I don't think they're in harm's way if we go up with the elevator and they immediately shut it off."

"What if we get overwhelmed and need to leave?" Milo shuts down my train of thought. "On top of that, if they leave the elevators on, the Demons could get in there and travel down to them. There would be no stopping them from coming down."

"We're getting ahead of ourselves," Stella interrupts. She turns to the girl and clears her throat. "You need to evacuate the premises immediately."

The girl looks concerned. "We wouldn't get our pay."

"Is your pay or your life more important to you right now?"

The girl sighs and goes into the lobby. Pretty soon, the whole staff is outside and evacuating. They tell us how to turn the elevators back on and how to lock the doors when we're done.

"Alright," Stella announces, "problem solved."

"That can't stop them from just leaving though, right?" I say.

Z shrugs. "I guess it can't, but we could always lock the doors to go outside at the bottom."

"But that just leaves us with the overwhelmed thing again," Stella sighs.

"I say we just take this and run with it," I say. "If something goes wrong, we could always find a place to hide, or just unlock the doors."

We turn to Milo, waiting for his input.

"Let's go, then," he announces, smiling despite the situation.

We go into the lobby then into a worker section from a side door and turn on the elevators. There doesn't seem to be any indicator, so I imagine the Raveners up high don't know, either. Then, we lock the doors behind us.

"Ready?" Z asks us.

We step into the elevator and press a button to go. I won't say that the scenic view calmed my nerves, but it was nice to see all of Seattle as we rode to one of the most dangerous things we've faced. I gulp as the elevator dings and the doors slide open.

The inside of the tower is very nice, actually a lot better condition than I thought for Demons inhabiting the area. The carpeted floor stretched across the observation deck, two doors leading out to the slanted glass that lets you see a better view of the city. I notice a staircase leading down to another floor.

I step out of the elevator and palm my knife, surprisingly excited to use it. I never really liked the Goph Guns, they were loud and hard to control. What if I didn't want to severely damage my enemy, like that night with Milo? If I didn't have a knife, I don't know if we both would have survived that encounter.

We start following the curve of the lookout, finding an abandoned cafe and a few things left from other guests, like phones, hats, and wallets. Maybe if we survive the fight we could put them in lost and found. The light from the sun lights our way as we search. We go back to the elevator, no Demons on our hands.

"This seems to happen every time," Milo points out. "We get somewhere, look around, don't find anything, and then they sneak up on us or something. Lucifer better not show up again."

"True," Z agrees, "but we still have a whole other level to search. If Lucifer was here, he would probably make it known."

With that, we travel to the staircase and start our descent. The stairs are pointing toward a wall, so we go down slowly. I grip my knife tighter and look behind me in the cracks of the stairs.

I see a group of Raveners, about ten in total, pacing around the hall. They haven't seemed to notice us yet, so I crouch down and shift down the stairs slower. My friends notice what I'm doing, look behind them as well, and copy my movements. I get to the bottom of the stairs and turn to my group.

"We should try and sneak up on each one individually," I whisper, my voice barely heard. "Maybe they won't notice us until it's too late."

They nod and we ease toward the group. We each split off and find our own Ravener to deal with.

I come up on one that is making its way toward one of the information booths. It's the size of a regular human, just slightly larger and gray, and with a slithering bottom half. It doesn't notice me as I sneak up behind it.

Our professor for the Ravener class, Ms. Peterson, didn't mention anything about extremely thick skin, so I assume that it would be easy to stab the thing in the heart, also assuming that it's in the same place as a human heart is. I lunge up silently and shove the knife between the place a human rib would be, and it slides right through, straight to the heart. The Ravener gurgles a bit and collapses. I can't stop the sound it makes as it drops to the floor and its blank eyes look up at me.

I tense, waiting for another Ravener to come check the noise out, but nothing comes. I frown, inspecting the Ravener lying on the ground in front of me and finding no ears.

Could the Raveners hear? Is that why they didn't notice us right away, because they can't hear us approaching? If so, Ms. Peterson obviously wasn't the best teacher.

I wait for a couple of seconds and proceed farther down the hallway. I see another Ravener approaching, so I quickly duck behind another information panel. The Ravener doesn't notice me as it travels farther down the hallway. I wait for it to pass my panel and tiptoe towards him. Something stops me before I can kill it, though, probably curiosity.

It enters the area where I killed the first Ravener. It makes a screeching noise upon seeing its dead friend and starts beating his worm tail rapidly against the ground, making it shake. The impact causes the glass on the ground to break, leaving gaping holes where visitors could stand on to see the floor below.

I gulp and immediately plunge my knife into the Ravener's heart, this time a little clumsily from adrenaline and being tired. The Ravener falls to the ground as answering screeches echo down the halls. About three Raveners come barreling from both directions of the hall, all followed by my friends from a distance. The Raveners don't seem to notice them, but they notice me, and they immediately come slithering towards me at their top speed.

Not knowing what to do, I stand stock still, frozen in terror. I decide to turn to the right, where there's only one Ravener, Z right behind it. I run towards it, throwing all my force into my feet as I flail my arms around, hoping to confuse it. My tactic miraculously works, but only for a split second. In this second of confusion, Z lunges forward at the thing and shoves his dagger into its heart. It collapses in a heap and I hop over its big, bulky body. The other Raveners are coming full force, and I have a feeling that the tactic won't work again, and it's now seen me and Z, so we bolt down the hallway.

We circle fully around to the stairs, and I start staggering up. Z doesn't seem to get the memo, though, because he continues his run around the hallway. One Ravener follows me and another one follows him, Stella chasing after the Ravener coming toward the stairs and Milo taking the Ravener on Z's heels.

I bolt up the stairs as fast as I can, the slithering Ravener following me up. Running to the doors leading outside, I shove them open and I'm on the balcony, wind whipping around me. I turn around, hoping to distract the Ravener. I slowly back up to the glass overlooking Seattle.

The Ravener looks like it thinks it's won, smiling wide as he opens its big, gaping mouth. I stare in horror at the over-extended teeth and tongue, coming closer to swallow me. I start to panic now.

"Stella!" I shout. "Any time would be super great!"

"My gun won't shoot!" She screams in frustration as the Ravener gets closer to me.

"Heads!" I screech, throwing it handle-down over the Ravener.

The Ravener almost swallows me whole but stops suddenly. It closes its mouth and tips toward me. I yelp and scramble out of the way as it crashes through the glass, tumbling to the earth below. I look over the ledge and watch as it impacts the ground, a big BOOM resounding up to us.

"You okay?" Stella asks after a second.

"Fine," I assure. "Come on, let's go make sure they have the other one taken care of."

We scramble away from the ledge and bolt to the steps, but not before a looming shadow falls over us. I stop in my tracks, but Stella keeps running. She's down the stairs before I can say anything, disappearing from sight.

I whirl to my right, bringing my knife out in front of me. Lucifer appears there, staring at me from a few yards away. I gulp and try to back towards the stairs, but a cold feeling washes over me that makes me immediately step away. I can feel tears coming to my eyes.

"Why?" I ask him, whisper quiet, still kind of shocked from the Ravener and still confused why he would do this to us. I was tired of him showing up and ruining everything.

This meant that we wouldn't be Hunters anymore, that we would have our memories erased, and that we won't even know each other. The one time I finally feel accepted, and it's ripped away from me.

Then, thinking about that, I felt angry.

"Why?" I say louder this time.

"Because we need your help." He says this like it pains him.

"With what?" I scream. "What could you possibly need help with from four teenagers? Adolescents! We've barely been on this earth for sixteen years. Why us? WHY? We won't even know each other because of you! YOU!"

He swallows hard, and looks away from me. "There's a Banshee in Kirkland, just eleven miles northeast of here. You need to go take care of it without your friends. They will be trapped down there until you come back, the job finished."

I'm crying now, anger making me delusional, staring at him. "I can't even drive," I finally say.

"I apologize."

I don't respond. With no other option, I walk toward the elevators. I stop before them, though, looking back slightly.

I make a decision, then. I would not let this guy ruin everything. "Don't hurt them."

"I won't."

I drove to Kirkland, finding a hole in the Barrier pretty quickly in the area of the Space Needle, big enough for the van to fit through, just barely. I was surprisingly good at driving, somehow getting the hang of it after I ran into a fire hydrant close to the Space Needle. I had to work quickly so that I could get back before anybody figured anything out. I was planning on not telling the Academy about Lucifer, it would just make things a ton of a lot worse than they already were.

I almost cried when I realized Kirkland didn't have a Barrier around it after looking it up online, and I realized how much the Barriers protected us as I was driving toward Kirkland, a bunch of Demons wandering around the long-ago abandoned buildings and roads. They tried to chase after me, but the van was too fast. A very terrifying experience driving for the first time.

I drove on a road that had a big sign reading 'Kirkland' at about two thirty. I scoured the city for a bit, surprisingly no Demons any-where. The old city was right beside the ocean, the water curving into the city slightly, with houses and buildings overlooking it. I wondered what it would have been like to live here all those decades ago, maybe watching the ocean, maybe going to a cafe. It made me realize how not much had changed since then, besides the whole demon and ghost situation.

We still had phones, and cafes, and the Space Needle, although space travel kind of came to a halt since then. I'm not sure why. I would think it would increase ten-fold. Maybe we could be living on a different planet, away from all these demons and ghosts and whatever. It also made me think about how to explain the whole spiritual side of it. Where even was the Underworld? The center of the earth? Then where did that make heaven, or whatever they call it. In the sky? That wouldn't make sense, though, since we've literally gone beyond our sky and there's a bunch of other solar systems and planets and stars and a ton more than just us.

A screeching stopped my thoughts completely. The sound seemed to stop everything around me, too, because the sound of the waves seemed to cease and my van also stopped completely. I tried to turn it back on again, but nothing. Sighing, and almost crying again, I opened the car door and went to the back of the van. I opened it up and grabbed the Phor, and closed it again. I made sure the van was in park, because the last thing I'd want would be to have an unusable van as well as a dead one, and set off toward where the sound came from.

Now, I'm stalking down a street, scared out of my mind, and tightening my grip on my knife. I just want this Banshee to show itself so I can get my friends and go back to the Academy. But what would happen then? Would we go to our next assignment and see Lucifer again and again until the end of it all? Why did he even need our help, anyway? Would we lie to the Councilors like they're lying to us about something? What were they even lying to us about? Why was everything so complicated? Why couldn't it just be black and white? Why can't I just have a normal life and be a normal teenager? Why is everything so unbelievably unfair?

A voice cuts me from my thoughts, a voice screaming for help. Even worse, I recognize this voice.

This voice is my father's.

My heart seems to stop as I sprint toward the direction of the voice. A small, rational part of me is telling me there is no way that my dad could be out here, and that it's probably the Banshee playing tricks on me. If I remembered correctly from the demons and ghosts sheet, Banshees mimic the sound of your loved ones' voices in order to lure you in. The much bigger, much less rational part of my brain is screaming at me to run faster, so I do.

I run as fast as I possibly can to an alley. My dad isn't there, just a dumpster with trash overflowing from it. I frown, and then I hear my dad's voice again, this time from behind me. I whip around as fast as I can, but there's nothing there. I dash out into the street, determined to find him and make sure he's safe.

Nothing.

I start to panic. My dad's scream comes again, seeming to be retreating from the street. The little rational part of my mind screams at me to stop again, but it sounds so real. Of course, I've never heard my dad in that much agony, but I imagine it would sound a lot like that.

I run toward my dad again. My feet are pounding against the pavement, in rhythm with my fast, erratic heartbeat.

"Dad!" I shout. "Dad, where are you?"

His screaming stops. I halt as silence fills the street and my mind immediately jumps to the worst. I somehow run faster. Imagine if Coach could see you now, a distant part of me thinks.

I turn the corner to where my dad's voice was coming from. Nothing. Nobody. A sob climbs up my throat.

Where did he go? Was he even here in the first place? Did I just walk into a trap? Yes, probably. I just walked into a trap willingly. As soon as I think this, I turn and bolt, but not before a multitude of voices start up.

My dad, my mom, Milo, Z, Stella, everyone I've ever loved, even Beanie's bark, they all start wailing and screaming for my help. The voices seem to come from everywhere all at once. I drop to my knees and cover my ears, to no effect because of my helmet, as the voices rise higher and higher in volume. I start screaming with them, tears streaming down my face.

It gets so bad that my ears start ringing, my vision blacks out, and I can feel a trickle of blood in my ears. I drop completely to the floor, curling up into a ball. The voices stop suddenly. I don't want to open my eyes to the world yet, so I keep them squeezed shut.

I feel a form over me, and somehow I know it's the Banshee. I can feel its soul slowly slipping into my body, but I press the button on the Phor quickly. Another round of screams come, even louder than before. I sob and curl into an even tighter ball until it stops. Then I take off my helmet, sit up, and vomit in the street.

After crying for a little bit longer in the street, rocking back and forth in the fetal position, and collecting myself and my stuff, I get up and start walking to my van, my helmet still off. I find it where I left it, parked by the ocean, still not turning on. I almost lie down and start sobbing again, but I pick myself up and look up why it couldn't be turning on online. It says it has a dead battery. I open the hood and look around inside. Sure enough, the battery box looks busted. I sigh and start searching for one in the city. After walking around for a while I find an old car shop named "All Wheel Drive Auto." I'm filled with relief when I find a battery that looks almost exactly like the one in the van.

I grab it and take off toward the van. I hope that the car accepts batteries from the 40s when I get there, and I open up the hood again. After a quick look online, I switch the batteries. I try the engine and it fires up. I smile a huge smile and immediately peel out of Kirkland, starting my journey back to Seattle.

The van doesn't drive as well as before, but it gets the job done. I hope I don't blow up from the old battery as I swerve around some demons. I get to the barrier after a bit, and look at the time. It's almost four, and I prepare myself for a reprimand from my parents as I slip through the hole in the barrier and pull back up to the Space Needle.

I get to the top and the elevator doors open with a ding. I step out and find Lucifer in the same spot, staring at me. I stumble toward him.

"I let your damn Banshee pass on," I say.

He looks at me for a second. Tilts his head and takes me in. He's probably looking at my bloody ears and tear-stained face. I hope he feels guilty, but, then again, he's a demon. He doesn't feel guilt. He says nothing as he waves his hand and shadows fall away from the entrance to the stairs.

My friends are there, sitting in the stairwell, their helmets off. When they realize the shadows are gone, they jump up and charge toward Lucifer. They stop short when they see me, though.

I must look really bad, because they just gape at me. Then Milo steps forward and wraps his arms around me. I somehow start to cry more, burying my head in his shoulder. I hug him tightly, and Stella and Z come forward, also wrapping their arms around me.

Finally, once I've stopped crying, Milo pulls away from me. "What happened to you?" he asked softly.

I just shake my head and turn to Lucifer.

He was staring at me, his face blank.

I stared back.

"What are you going to do now?" he asked. It wasn't condescending like I expected, it wasn't reprimanding, he seemed like he genuinely wanted to know.

It gave me pause.

What was I going to do?

I couldn't go back to the Academy with blood in my ears and not have them ask questions, and I knew that if I went back, even with my ears not bloody, I'd have to either lie to them and see Lucifer again and again or tell the truth and get my memory wiped. It seemed like no matter what I did, it would end badly. For everyone involved.

Plus, even if I did go back to the Academy, I'm not sure I could trust any of the Councilors, and I might not even be able to trust Alexander. They were lying to us about something, but what?

"Do you know what the Councilors are lying about?" I ask Lucifer.

He pauses. "Yes."

"Tell us."

"In order to do that you would need to join us."

That makes me think too. What if my options aren't black and white. What if it's not a matter of whether I should lie to the Councilors or not, but what if it's a matter of if I should even be on the Councilors' side? What if I've been fighting for the wrong reasons? What if Lucifer isn't lying? What if he actually needs our help with something only we can help him with?

I stare at him. Something must change in my expression, because his shoulders seem to loosen. Then I look at my friends.

"What if," I start, voicing my thoughts, "what if we're looking at this all wrong. What if Lucifer is telling the truth?"

Z's mouth drops. "Rain, are you listening to yourself? Lucifer, the Lucifer, you think he's telling the truth? What do you mean?"

"What if we're fighting for the wrong team? Don't you guys get it? They're lying to us! My dad always tells me that the world isn't always black and white, good and evil. What if the demons aren't evil? What if we are?"

"Rain, what happened to you out there?" Stella puts her head to my forehead like I have a fever. "Are you okay?"

"You aren't listening!" I shout, pulling away from her. "Milo, please." I turn to him. "You're smart! You're logical! Please, just think for a second. Think about what I said. Think about everything that has happened so far."Milo stops. His brow furrows and he looks at his feet. I breathe hard. It seems like a century passes before he speaks again.

"She's right," Milo whispers. "At least, something isn't right with the Academy. Something is happening, and I don't think it's anything good. They're lying to us, you guys."

"You can't be serious," Z says weakly.

"No," Stella mumbles, "just because they're lying to us about a small thing doesn't mean they're the bad guys. They're not."

"Think about it, you two. They've been keeping things from us since we got here. Nobody even knows for sure what happened in the Outbreak of the Underworld. Do you?"

"What does that have to do with anything?" Stella shouts.

"Just answer the question," Milo says calmly.

"Okay, fine," Z sighs. "The demons came out of some mountain range or whatever and attacked nearby cities unprovoked."

"Did Alexander say unprovoked, though?" Milo answers.

Z pales. "I...I don't know."

Stella gulps. "What does bad memory have to do with this? So what if Alexander forgot to say unprovoked. This doesn't prove anything."

"Okay," Milo says, "what about when we first went to the Councilors? When Alexander said we should be careful what we say to them?""What are you suggesting?" she growls.

"I'm suggesting that Alexander knows something he's not telling us. I'm suggesting that Rain is right. I'm suggesting that maybe we should reconsider our options here."

A look of defeat passes her face. Then disbelief. Then anger. Then back to defeat. "I don't entirely believe you, but I guess you're right."

A couple of seconds of silence. Then, Z speaks again.

"So, what now?"

We all turn to Lucifer. He's just watching us, his arms crossed in front of him. "Well, are you joining us or what?"

"I guess we are," Rain remarks.

We walk out of the Space Needle with lucifer. I can't quite believe what's happening, but I hope we're making the right choice. He told us that we would have to go back to the Academy for the week and pretend that everything was fine. He used some of his shadow-power stuff on me and there's no ringing in my ears anymore.

"So, what now?" Z asks.

"You wait until your next assignment," Lucifer answers. "If you can't wait until then, or if something goes wrong, run away. If you press this button," he holds out a device to us, "I'll come get you."

Milo takes the device.

"Good luck, TU Crew," Lucifer says as he sinks back into the shadows.

We stare at the place where he was for a second. Then, Milo holds up his wrist. "Are you all okay?"

"Could be better," Stella mumbles, still looking pale, "but I'll survive. We've still got each other, right?"

"Right," I say, wrapping my arm around her.

Milo makes a portal to Ecsporavet and looks back at us.

"No turning back now," he says.

"Trust me, we know," Z remarks. "Let's go lie to these Councilors."

I'm not sure what the future holds, or if we will even be able to escape IDHS, but I know that I have my friends.

If that's not enough, then I don't know what is.